The Realm

Painter

"This is how you do it: You sit down at the keyboard and you put one word after another until it's done. It's that easy, and that hard."

- Neil Gaiman

Acknowledgments

My boyfriend: Carlos Barraza

My friends: Keiko and Gretel:

My Teachers: Mrs. Dipeppe (English

teacher) & Mr. Carter (Art teacher)

and of course you. The very

thoughtful person who picked up my

book and decided to give it a chance.

A special thanks to all of you. This

book wouldn't be possible without

you.

Author Signature

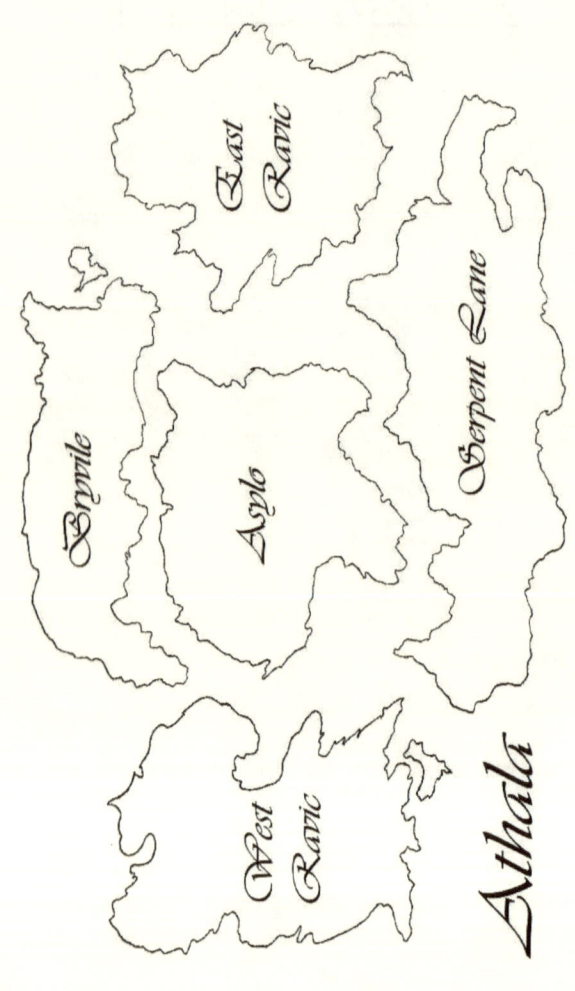

<u>Chapter 1</u>

December 6th, 2201

"Happy Birthday Uvania!" my family says to me in unison at the table.

I hear a plate being placed down in front of me. The scent of pancakes with maple syrup greets my nose. They are hot and very much ready for me to dig into them. I can't wait to taste their fluffy goodness.

"I made your favorite breakfast for your special day." my mom points out.

"Thanks, mom but there's no reason to spoil me. I'm only turning seventeen. Really, it's no big deal," I stuff a pancake in my mouth "These are delicious. You're such a good cook."

"Nonsense. Your birthday is always going to be important your my first child, my only girl, and a very smart one at that."

"She's right," my dad chimes in with his deep voice. I hear him adjust his newspaper "You will always be my little girl. My only girl no matter how old you get."

"I'll always be here you know. You still have me. You know Menic, your son. Who by the way would also like breakfast." my younger brother points out sounding a bit envious.

"Don't worry son we haven't forgotten

about you." my father reassures him with a nice hard pat on the back.

"Uh huh sure." Menic says with his mouth stuffed.

"So Uvania do you have any plans for today? Any ideas on how you will be celebrating." my brother says to me smiling.

I feel everyone's eyes on me when he asks that question. My head falls so I'm looking at my pancakes. I know the answer they want me to give them. Truth be told I don't have the type of plans they want. However, I do have plans to enjoy myself. Even if it's the same thing I do every day.

"No," I say lifting my head up "I was just going to sit home and finish my painting Rebirth."

"But you paint every day." my mom says aloud with a bit of sorrow in her voice. She got her hopes up.

"Well, mom I can't help but do what I love. The fact that I get to do what I have a passion for with every passing second is a blessing." I explain to her.

"You can't even -" she catches herself mid-sentence.

Silence falls upon the room. Tension feels the air.

"What...I can't even *see* what I'm painting. It's okay to say it, mom. I was born blind. It's not like I know any different. I can't see. However, when my paintings are dry I can feel the brushstroke patterns. I can feel the different layers. I can feel the painting that I imagined in my head." I say calmly.

I hear my mom's footsteps get lighter and lighter. She must've left the room. It kills her on the inside when she makes mistakes like this. She's still not use to my lack of ability to see even though I was born this way. Yet she still makes the mistake. I'm sure she's even harder on herself right now for bringing it up on my birthday.

"She'll be fine." Menic says.

"I know." I state while continuing to eat my pancakes.

The chair on my right makes a cacophonous scratching noise across the floor. It's then followed by a plop and air being released from the cushion.

10

Menic just moved closer to me if I know better.

"Well, I guess there's no time like the present then." He says to me.

He takes the fork and knife out of my hand. Slides the plate away from both of us. Then he takes my hands and places them both palm side up flat against the table in front of me. It's then followed by a light pressure. A birthday present. A smile runs across my face.

"We all chipped in to get you something special. I helped mom and dad pick out the right gift so don't worry." he says with a lighthearted smile.

I giggle in response to this. My brother seems to understand me the most. We always got along. To be honest, wouldn't want it any other way. We share so many jokes together no one could ever replace or forget about him.

I feel the box in my hands. I find the edges taking in all its dimensions. Shaking it lightly up and down I hear the contents on the inside shift firmly in place. My hands find their way to the bow that has huge curls.

"Go ahead open it. I want to see the smile on your face when you open it." he says to me in a happy tone of voice.

I rip it open and remove the plastic I can find. I run my hands over the surface and I feel it. Some of it is smooth other parts which seem to have caps have many ridges.

"It's an introductory set of Gamblin Oil paint tubes. I had to do my research, but I think I did a good job."

My face lights up. I raise my hand to find his face. He places my right hand on his left cheek. From this position, I now know how I can hug him. I throw my arms around him and a few tears run down my face.

"This is literally the best gift ever. It's perfect your amazing. I can't wait to try them out." I say excitedly wiping the tears from my face.

"Come on let's test them out now. I'll walk you to your room."

"Oh, just hold on you two. Before you go heading off at least blow out the candles on the cake your mom made you." my dad says to us.

"Alright." my brother answers.

Once again, I hear feet hitting the ground closer this time. I guess my mom decided to come back and join us. She can be quite predictable at times. This is one of them.

"Thanks for coming back, Janet. Uvania was just about to blow out the candles on her beautiful birthday cake." he tells her.

I hear plastic being shifted towards me. *Flick, flick, flick.* That's all I hear. That and Menic's breathing. This is going to be a memorable moment. Mostly for my mom but a memorable moment none the less. Though it might be seen as silly for a person turning seventeen years old. I still make a wish for my birthday, every year.

"Alright baby girl, blow out the candles."

"Don't forget to make a wish" Menic instructs.

"Trust me I won't." I smile.

"Before you do I want to at least tell you what the cake looks like," my mom begins "Okay so it's a rectangular two layered cake. Vanilla, of course. White icing with pink as an outline. It reads happy seventeen we love you. Okay now blow out the candles."

"A.k.a don't spit on it." he giggles.
I let out a small laugh. That's my brother for you. Goofy at every opportunity. I blow out the candles and wish for my sight. Or to be more specific I wish to be able to see. Anything. Maybe even everything. I just want my eyes to work.

A fine thread of smoke finds its way to my nostrils. Hoping I got them all I sit back in my chair and let out a small sigh of relief. Contemplating if my wish will ever come true. Who's to say it will or won't.
"So, what'd you wish for?" my mother burst out.

"I can't tell you." I say in a fake and theatrical tone "If I told you that it wouldn't come true." I point out.

14

"I'm your mother of course you can."

"You're my baby girl, of course, you can."
"Sorry guys but this birthday. This birthday wish I'm keeping under lock and key." I say firmly.

"So, to your room then?" my brother says to cue our exit.
"To my room." I say excitedly.

"Okay, I'll carry the box of paints."
He takes my hands placing one on each of his broad shoulders. My hands feel like there in a higher position than usual. His shoulder sturdier than before.

"Menic you're getting taller again. What are you like five seven now?" I ask him.
"Not yet but I'm getting there."

We start walking. Following directly in line with my brother's footsteps. I go silent for a moment. I wonder why he does this. He doesn't have to.
"You don't have to do this you know. I have the layout of the house memorized."

"I know, but I did it so often when we were

younger I started to enjoy it. Can't really explain it. Plus, you're my big sister I like to think I can help you too. You help me with everything. Girls, school, you even get me out of trouble with our parents sometimes. When I walk you around the house every now and again I actually feel like I'm doing something. That I'm helping you in some weird way. I know you don't need me. But sometimes I'd like to think you do." Menic explains.

"What are you doing? Getting all soft on me now are you." I say in a happily and a bit choked up.

"Come on sis' you know it's true. Don't go crying on me either. You'll make me cry."

We both laugh. Menic comes to a slow before we both stop. He turns and looks at me. I can feel it. My hands fall to my sides. I give him a curious look and tilt my head to the side.

"I'm curious. What did you wish for?"

My eyes fall to the floor once again and I start to twiddle my fingers. Feeling a bit guilty on the inside I allow myself to tell him. Out of our entire family, he is the only one who can handle this type of truth.

I whisper, "I wished for the ability to see."

"Why would you do that?" he questions.

"I don't know. I'm insecure I guess. Feels like I'm missing out on life a bit. Plus, I get tired of hearing mom or others stumble over the words they say. Sometimes it's just annoying. Sometimes I feel like I'm a bit of a burden."

"Uvania," Menic says as he holds both my shoulders firmly "You are the most perfect person I know. Your sight is freaking amazing. You notice things before I do. You get better grades. You handle people well. You are everything I aspire to be in life. You're perfect. Honestly, I can't even imagine you any other way. The fact that your blind makes you all the more unique. So, don't say things like that," he tucks some of my hair behind my ear "You are my big sister after all."

"Alright enough. I get it I say. Let's get to painting." I walk into my room Menic close behind. "I'll put the paints in the corner until you finish this painting. You'll have to test them when you finish this one. I wouldn't want you messing up this one. I really like it."

I take a seat on my floor as usual. I keep everything in the same spot that way I don't forget where each color is. Everything laid out before me in a semi-circle. Oil paints, brushes, canvas, palette, and mediums.

"I like the idea of the girl floating in the shallow water with a butterfly in the center of her chest. I also like the way you positioned her hands. Her fingertips towards the butterfly. Have you figured out a name for the painting yet by the way?"

"I said it earlier remember, Rebirth."

"Right, right. Nice I like it."

"What don't you like?"

"Pizza with pineapples."

I burst into laughter.

I hear Menic place the paints on the floor. He then comes and takes a seat next to me. I start painting Rebirth. Grabbing my brushes and dipping it in scarlet red and start painting the lips of the subject. Frequently I go back and forth imagining myself adding fine details in. Though I'll truly never know.

<u>Chapter 2</u>

"Alright Uvania its curfew. You've officially been painting 5 consecutive hours. I think it's time to deem yourself a little break."

"Already I was so busy being engulfed and consumed by my own art I totally didn't notice the time passing. Well it's all in a days work right."
"If you say so. You're the artist after all. Well I'm going to head out and catch some z's."

"Alright night Menic" I call out.
I get up from my spot and head over to my bed and

pull the covers over myself. Benefit of being blind. I never have to worry about light preventing me from going to sleep or burning my eye sockets at day break. Falling asleep within minutes. Then strangely enough I felt my body intensely vibrating. Nowhere similar to a seizure but my insides where definitely thrashing uncontrollably. Then it stops. Feeling light as air I feel myself coming out of my body. What's happening.

"Somebody help! I'm floating away."
Looking at my floating form of some type of a spiritual body. It's made of what seems to be electricity. What is going on? This is freaking me out. I'm literally outside of my body. I freeze in place and become more confused than before. There's no sound. Or movement. Everything just exist.

I get slammed back into my body hard. It hurts like a body being trapped in walls closing in on me. Bone crushing torture. You could say it was bone chilling in a way. Soon after a tingling follows, and I begin to dream.

My eyes flicker open. My body in something soft, liquid like, I'm floating. A river delta? Where am I? Moving my arms away from my chest a butterfly makes the decision to take flight. I tread the water and glance around. What is all this? I can see. The water. . .it's. . .blue and gray. At least that's how it makes me feel. Is this real? Am I actually having a dream right now. This is a first. Filled with vivid colors. A dream come true. I watch the ripples travel the water intensely enjoying all of it. Storing it in my memory.

The trees are an array of textures with their bumpy and cracked brown trunks. Blooming into tiny little leaves that look like the size of quarters from here. I tilt my head up and stare at the sky above me. Stunning blues, yellows, and hints of oranges. Am I experiencing a sunset? Is it summer? The wind howls and whistles and I notice leaves tumbling away in the winds followed by titanium white clouds coming in. That's strange.

Then again, I'm in a dream where I have 20/20 vision. It doesn't get any stranger than that. Who cares I'm happy. When I stop staring at the forest area so hard I find my eyes being drawn towards a dock. It seems to be made of old rotting wood. Still usable though. More over to the left of the dock there's a rope hanging from a tree. Must be used for a swing for people to throw themselves in the water. I always wanted to try that, but I was always too scared.

Can I just stay here forever and enjoy the luke warm water wrapping around my body from the collar bone down. The sight that I always wanted. I'm literally in my happy place. I would give anything to stay here for eternity.

"I really do want to stay forever." I say smiling while looking at my reflection in the water.

That's when something deep down beneath the surface grabs me by the ankle and pulls me. I can't catch my breath. I begin choking on the water and soon there is no light able to be seen from where I'm at. What's happening? I struggle as my heart bangs against my chest.

My lungs. . .they need air. . .breathe.

<u>Chapter 3</u>

"Uvania it's time for breakfast." Menic calls from the kitchen.

"Don't worry I'm coming."

"Alright."

I get out of my soft and comfortable bed and stretch my entire body. My shoulder makes a small popping noise. That felt good. Making my way to the kitchen I feel excited. Not just because I smell pancakes probably left over from yesterday. But I get to tell my family about the dream I had.

I wonder what they'll think. Not only did I have my first dream. It was a normal dream and not the auditory dreams I hear blind people have every now and then.

"So, did everyone sleep well last night?" my dad questions trying to be the conversation starter. "I had an awesome dream last night. I won the most votes for the most valuable player on my basketball team. It was awesome. A few more games at school and maybe I can finally make it a reality. Right now, at school me and Kyle seem to be tied."

"Sounds cool." I say.

My mom follows up with "Speaking of I finished laundry yesterday. So, your jerseys and shorts are now clean."

"Thanks mom you're the best."

"I had a dream too." I say getting a bit nervous out of nowhere.

"You did?" my mom says bamboozled.

I hear a fork fall and hit a plate somewhere. The only other sound in the room is the coffee brewing. This was supposed to be an exciting and fun thing to tell them. Why did they get all quiet? It feels awkward now. Did their mouths fall open too?

"Really! Cool tell us about it." Menic says urging me for all the details.

"It was amazing. There was this huge river delta that I was swimming in that was miles upon miles long. Nearby there was this long dock and it was a light brownish color. The sky was all these different shades of colors with clouds scattered in it. There where these amazing trees that were like ten feet tall. The leaves were a dark green and they spread out really far. I mean I definitely don't think I was here in Arizona at all. But it was beautiful." I explain to Menic.

"How did you. . .I mean?" my mom stutters over her words.

"Well that's just great honey." my father says conflictedly.

"How did you know the colors?" my brother asks in my mom's place of not being able to speak.

"Not sure, it just felt right. It's like the dream I had just came with the knowledge. The background information. When I saw the colors, I didn't even think about it I just knew. It was all just so natural to say the sky was mixed with pastel yellows, orange, and pinks and purples. It felt even more natural to say the water was deep blue and gray type of color. It was a dream, so I just went with it." I state.

"Is this the first time you've had a dream like this?" my brother asks.

"Yeah. I hope I get to have another dream like that."

"Me too. It seems to have made you really happy. Your cheeks are turning pink from how much your smiling."

"Are you telling the truth or are you just teasing me with this story?" my mother says out of nowhere.

"Janet!" my dad screams.

She said it with no hesitation. No wavering in her voice. This was all her. Even now it feels like she didn't regret it. How long had she been waiting to say this? Where has she found this new bravery?

Either way I should respond.

"No John, I'm serious. I'm sick of it. I have enough trouble as it is finding the right words to say. I haven't been able to find the right words for over a decade. I'm not going to let my own daughter sit there and tease me with some stories about how she can see in such dreams. I won't have it," my mom shouts loud enough for the neighbors to hear. "Janet Katherine Marie what has gotten into you?"

"Mom, please don't start." Menic jumps in with heavy dread in his voice.

"John, you know just as well as I it's not possible! Blind people do not have dreams that vivid. We don't even dream that vivid. We don't dream at all. People who are blind have auditory dreams. That's just the way it is. So, I'm not going to apologize or regret what I just said. I will not let my own child sit across from me and lie to me! I won't tolerate it."

"Janet! Where is this all coming from?"

"You know what you did!" she screams.

"What are you talking about?"

29

"You know what you did John."

"Menic what's going on?" I whisper.

"Your guess is about as good as mine." he states.

"Let's get out of here. Head outside maybe?" Menic gets up and then assists me in my walking. I assume he does this, so we can get out of the room faster. Whether we actually do get out in time is something that can be argued. What did I say that made her so angry like that? I just wanted to tell everyone about my happy experience. Yet somehow, I started a war?

We get outside and Menic and I decide to sit on the porches wooden steps. We are right outside the door, but the voices are trapped inside. I'm happy we didn't need to go any further than our own back porch.

"So, continue telling me about your dream." my brother tells me.

"Well I told you all of the amazing parts. I was going to tell you this later but since we're already talking by ourselves I'll tell you now. It wasn't a dream Menic. Not at all. It was something else. I'm not a hundred percent sure. But before I started dreaming this weird thing happened. I felt my body buzzing and I became like pure floating energy or something. I was out of my body and I saw myself."

"You saw yourself?" he says "What does that even mean Uvania?"

"You know. How I look. Long black silky hair, pink lips, small round face." I start listing off details.

"I see." he says in an odd tone.

"What is it?" I say sounding a little disappointed.

"Nothing, I just," he trails off.

"You just what?" I urge him to continue.

"I just don't believe in that sort of thing."

"But it happened. I'm telling you the truth. I've never lied to you and I'm not gonna start today. You have to believe me."

"Uvania it's not possible. There is no way that could ever happen." he says in a bored type voice.

"Then how else would you explain it?"

"Explain what?"

"How else would you explain me knowing my colors so well. What everything looked like. Explain it." I say getting upset at him.

"I can't."

"Then how can you tell me it didn't happen?"

"Cause it's not possible. Have you ever heard of anyone else having such an experience? No, because it never happened. It's not possible. Period."

"Well if you can't explain my experience. And you don't believe me why were you so interested to begin with inside. Explain that to me?"

"The answer to that question is simple. I was curious to know about your dream. But I didn't expect you to say something so farfetched. Plus, you're my sister." he tells me.

I stare at my brother blankly. It's like I almost don't recognize him. He's still Menic right? My little brother. We were thicker than thieves. He always had my back and now out of the blue sky he doesn't believe me. Since the day he was born we were inseparable and now he's turning his back on me. Maybe I am just jumping to conclusions or caught up in my emotions, maybe. However, if I let history speak for itself. I've never heard my brother talk like this.

Menic is standing right in front of me now. Less than two feet away with his tan skin. Nude pink lips forming a flat shape showing his genuine disinterest, he did not like continuing this topic of conversation. I couldn't see it. But I could feel it, more importantly I can hear it. The way his mouth formed his words was changing. Less enunciated and more mumbled and whisper like.

"Are you alright Uvania?" he looks at me a tad worried.

"You know I'm not really sure anymore." I say.

He places his hand on my right shoulder. It startles me a bit at first. I don't say anything I just listen.

"I believe you to an extent. That's all I can say." he tells me.

"What if I got you proof? What if I find someone who shares the same experience as me? Then would you believe me? Would you fully believe me then?"

"I mean... I guess I would have to believe you. I doubt you can find that type of proof. Anyway, it seems like the yelling and the spewing of venomous insults has begun to settle. Sounds like it's safe to go inside now," he pats me on the shoulder twice "See ya inside big sis."

I hear his footsteps and the door shut behind him.

"Big sis? What?" I whisper to myself.

After making that comment I head in myself a few minutes later. As usual I walk in my room and start gathering my new supplies provided by my brother. Who knew I would have a new idea for a painting so soon. Not to mention I'd be using Gamblin's oil paints to do so I think to myself.

I curse myself every now and again for dropping my brushes or losing my train of thought. Letting my frustration get the best of me. Yelling so loudly in my head that my lungs burn anyway. Every so often I also have to remind myself to take a deep breath and breathe. I'm slowly but surely going mad.

You can't blame me, can you? I know what I saw. What I experienced. What I dreamt. It was literally as clear as day. Oh my god I'm talking to myself. Why am I talking to myself? Maybe there right I am going crazy. No, I'm certain I experienced it. Oh no I'm giving myself a headache. Stop thinking.

My thoughts start unraveling at the seams faster than I can patch them back together. What's going on? How did this all start? How did it all start with me, a wish, and a dream. Please tell me.

No one can though. It's all just my imagination apparently if my own brother doesn't even believe me. My dream may have been just a dream. But that dream is causing me to live a nightmare I did not ask for. Maybe that's why people tell you to be careful what you wish for. Even if there was something I could do. There's just no way fathomable that this genie would go back in its bottle.

If there was an actual genie behind this I would love to trap it in a container and shake it back and forth until it agrees to first give me a reasonable and elaborate explanation and then make it as if this all never happened. Only if. Only if.

<u>Chapter 4</u>

Finally, after calming down all the ruckus in my brain all is well. Well, better than it was anyway. I'm finding my more Zen state of mind I guess you could say. Sitting in my semi-circle of art supplies can do that to an artist.

I imagine my painting only allowing myself to think and make artistic choices. Planning out a rough sketch in my head is how I've always done it. Should I make the background black, white, or gray? What angle should I put my subject at? Well it's a hybrid of a moth and a butterfly. So, it should be tilted and angled in a way, so the viewer can see its wings. What type of moth should I use? What type of butterfly should I use? Which should be on top and which should be on bottom? More importantly what color combination should I use?

I think the colors orange and green would work well. Sounds like a plan orange and green it is. Oh! Right, so should I be making this more abstract or conceptual? So many choices. Should I give it an impasto affect...no it doesn't fit. See this is why I don't use an outline. It would box me in and hold me back. I wouldn't be able to think as freely and spontaneously. I would end up holding myself to my underpainting. I need freedom to ramble off ideas. I need the oils to capture how impulsive I am. All my raw and natural ideas.

That said I start dipping my small paintbrush in a small amount of medium. After I dip my brush in oil paint and make the first stroke on canvas something comforts me on the inside. I feel warm fuzzies in my stomach. It makes me feel childlike and happy. Almost as if I had built the biggest pillow fort in all of history. Not just any pillow fort. It would be one made of the softest, whitest, and fluffiest feather pillows ever invented. It was *the* pillow fort.

I had only made a single stroke in the background area of the painting and my mind was already telling me that this could possibly be one of my best artwork pieces yet. This would be an art piece that I would have on my wall for my kids to see. For my kids to pass down. Maybe I was getting ahead of myself. Maybe I was getting a big head. But what can I say. I'm an artist, therefore I'm a dreamer. Let me dream. Let me dream in every color of the rainbow.

I continue painting the background and making decisions. Perspective will be the name of my new masterpiece. It will also be the distraction from my new-found reality. It can't be helped. My brother has made me feel like the odd ball out. My parents are bickering within themselves. They never argue. So, this is almost as otherworldly as my experience.

Perspective is a funny thing really. It's completely subjective to the eye of the beholder. Naming my painting Perspective might be a bit farfetched even for me. But that's what I picture so that's what I'll paint. I chose to combine the two for a good reason though. There is a method to my madness. By that I mean I've totally justified it. The same way I justify talking to myself and that I'm not going crazy. Butterflies and moths are in the same family. While moths may look a bit more earth toned and rough around the edges, butterflies are more pretty and gentle and don't try to attack my face in the late hours of the night because I still have my light on and window open. But I can't help it I have to keep my room highly ventilated.

There are many interesting things about moths and butterflies. If moths were people they'd be those family members that you don't really like to associate yourselves with. The family members that live out of state and only visit once every blue moon, so you don't think about them too much. Sometimes you even forget about them. You know until they come to town and visit and you're like oh yeah you exist. Nice to know your still alive.

Then when it comes to butterflies it's a completely different story. Butterflies are like your favorite cousins. They're full of energy and excited when they see you. You think you can take on the world. There the ones that you brag to your friends about. The one that you tell your secrets too. Butterflies are the ones you share those special moments with that you'll remember for a lifetime.

They're both insects with wings. They are both a force of nature. They are exactly the same. While being completely different. They are a living contradiction. An oxymoron if you will. Or at least they seem that way to me. So why not make them share a body together on canvas. Split right down the middle. Or something like it since I'm not making my brother use a ruler to be exact.

What will other people think of my painting?

What will they make of it? I think the question of my painting will be obvious. Is a butterfly a beautiful version of the moth? Or is the moth the ugly truth of the butterfly? I guess it's all just perspective.

<u>Chapter 5</u>

It's been three days, long days at that. I can't really handle all this. The yelling back and forth with my parents. My brothers acting. . .different. I haven't dreamt another dream since that day. Right now, it seems like I need a dream like that now more than ever. Take me far away to another place where such chaos does not exist. A safe haven of sorts.

    Perspective is finishing drying so maybe I'll start a new painting. I'll call it A new sound. Since my mind seems to only want to think of the one visual dream I had. I would make an entire painting dedicated to the dream world I once had. It has seemed to given my new life a new tune after all. That's it I'll just paint another painting. Then I'll be able to keep myself busy. Don't be so silly I remind myself. It will never be like the actual place. I wish I didn't have to call it a place. Actually, I should give it a name of its own. It's my world right so I can name it anything. Soon as I start thinking about possible names Menic sits beside me and lets out a deep breath.

"No one has told you anything I suppose. The only thing you know is that dad and mom are arguing. None of it makes any sense to you does it. Your smart, so I'm guessing you didn't have your ears pushed up against the wall trying to distinguish it either. Am I right?"

"Right, I guess?" I respond "Menic when did your voice get raspier?"

"Last night. Anyway, if I don't tell you you'll be in the dark forever so I'm just going to tell you what happened. Whether you believe it or not is up to you. I'm just passing the knowledge along alright?"

"Okay." I say firmly.

Menic is acting all distant again. I'd question him like a cop doing an interrogation but right now I want to see what information he provides willingly first. If I interrupt now he might just walk off on me. It seems like that's what the new Menic would do anyway.

"It was about a month ago. Everything was normal. Before all this bullshit started." he begins explaining as he takes out a cigarette and lighter "It was late at night and I was getting up for a late-night snack. I kept hearing noises. I thought it was just bumps in the night. At first, I just ignored it. But it kept getting louder. Eventually after trying to brush it off and actually getting a late-night bite, I decided to check it out. Which I'll point out now wasn't a smart decision. But you know what they say. Hind sight is always 20/20. I followed the noise to where I thought it was coming from. The door was open.

Wide open. The lights where on and everything.
That's when I saw it."

"Saw what?"

"Her," he says angrily with venom in his words "A
woman with long flowing red hair. Olive skin
glistening with body sweat. No clothes on draped all
over our father. She was pretty, but she wasn't our
mother. They stopped, and both looked at me. At
first the three of us were all in shock. So, she didn't
try to cover herself. But eventually we all gained
movement. The red head moved aside, and dad had
assured me that if I didn't say anything or tell anyone
everything would be fine. Just don't tell mom. He
promised he wouldn't cheat again and everything."

"So-"

"I believed him like a dumbass," he laughs it off with
a tone carrying sorrow and guilt "Can you believe it.
I actually bought that shit. He promised you know. I
looked up to him. Now look what's happened.
Weeks later here we are on the porch hiding outside
of our own home as our mother bitches him out for

46

it."

"Well that really sucks Menic. I'm sorry you walked in on that whole ordeal. It's not your fault. You were put in a hard position. I'm sure they'll work it out sooner or later right."

"I hope your right Uvania. I hope your right," he says to me "Well that's all I had to say on the matter."

I hear his foot stomp on the cigarette. I'm not sure if he's stomping out a cigarette he had no business having. Or pretending to step on the face of someone he thinks is the scum of the earth. Where is all this aggression coming from? Menic is a pacifist he literally wouldn't even hurt a fly. He literally catches them and puts them outside.

"Menic," I say wearily "You've been acting different lately. Is everything alright?"

"Peachy. Don't worry about it?"

"If somethings wrong you can tell me. Menic I'm worried about you."

"That's not my name," he says finally before I

hear his voice fade and feet rustling in the grass. He must be going for a walk into town.

Did he get involved with the wrong group of people at school. Did he need something more in life? Something to make his adrenaline flow smoother and pump harder. I thought I knew him. I thought I knew my parents too. If this week has proven anything it's that I know absolutely nothing at all. Like I've been in the dark my entire life.

I dust off the thought about my brother and resume the thoughts of what to name my dream world. It should be based on something I love right? So, what do I like? Daisies, cooking, Asian traditions, and art. Daisies merry-go-round, no. Even though it fits because that's how it feels sometimes, fresh and roller coaster like, it's to whimsical sounding. Uvania's summer escape, also fitting but not creative enough. Moments pass and then the name comes to me. Athala. I'll name it Athala it sounds pretty, and it's based off the often mispronunciation of my favorite oil color Pthalo blue.

The porch is my new favorite spot. It's a place to think, a place of revelation, and even inspiration. Not to mention it's outside the house so way more quiet and beautiful. It's nice, warm, and welcoming. Even though its December it's still warm. We do live in Arizona and snow will probably fall soon but growing up here I consider it warm.

Speaking of warmth, I'd really like to travel back to Athala. I wish I could travel there on a whim. I bet it's always warm there. I'm sure it never even rains. It's perfect and in a perfect world the weather is never subpar. I don't have any confirmation of that. Maybe I should follow my brother's advice. I should find someone who has experienced what I have. . .or at least something similar. There's always one person. The question is where should I start.

Chapter 6

I go to my room and pull out my laptop. I plop down on the bed with a firm thud. Placing my pc far enough in front of me that I can sit Indian style. The computer starts up and comes to the home screen with an annoying chime sound. Really wish someone would change the sound every once in a while. Try a sound that doesn't murder my ears.

Then I ponder on where I put my wireless mouse and stumble around searching for it taking minutes away from my goal, research. Gotcha! When

I find it, I move on to open google and start
researching. But when the google page is nice and
ready I end up with my blinker there disappearing
and reappearing. I'm not sure if I know how to type
everything I experienced into a few key terms.
"Now what?"

I start typing in randomness. "Dreaming of
seeing yourself out of your body." 17.7 million results
show up. That's too many so I read all the articles on
the first page alone. Most of them just talk about the
psychology behind it and how cool it is to have an
out of body experienced. A lot of people seem to
refer to it as OBE. Nothing of any use to me at the
moment.

I start a new search and type in "being able to see in
a dream when your blind." This search actually turns
up as twice as many results. All of them are wrong
because google changed it around to do blind people
dream. Or simply discusses the fact that we have
auditory dreams. Which is stuff that I've lived and
experienced first-hand, so I don't need google to

explain it to me.

Third times a charm. NOT! I type in "dreaming of being in your paintings." Even more results then the first result. It just gives me a ton of pages mentioning psychic revelations or dream interpretations. It's all irrelevant maybe this was a bad idea. Maybe if I accept the fact that I am indeed crazy this would all be easier.

"I'm not giving up."

I try a different method of research. I look at all groups on my social media that relates to empaths and astral projection. Maybe individual people will share a similar story or experience that they didn't necessarily want to post it on the web.

The first group I go to says it doesn't seem like any experience they've ever heard or experienced. Some just bluntly state that it's not even possible. Nonetheless they say if I have another experience I should share my progress with them.

Multiple groups and a few individual messages later I find more useless information. More people who want to be kept updated. More second guessing. The only thing I've learned is that I am terrible at researching.

All the reading and research I've gone through has burned time. Now having felt like I've wasted time and been completely unproductive I decide to work on my new art pieces underpainting in watercolor. At least when I paint I will definitely make progress opposed to getting more and more frustrated.

Though eventually I give up on that as well because I just can't keep my head screwed on straight with so much clutter in my brain.

<u>Chapter 7</u>

"Tell me why are we in school?" Kenzi asks me in lunch.

"Because the last four days have been teacher work days."

"So, they bring us back on a Friday! They might as well have given us the entire week off. Or at least us seniors. Sleep never killed anybody, and I could really use some." she complains as she unpacks her lunch from a brown paper bag.

"You should be happy we got four

consecutive days off to begin with."

"Maybe so," she states, "But I will never understand Marison Highschool."

"It's a good thing were seniors then. You don't have to keep wasting time attempting to figure it out."

"Agreed."

"So how was your weekend?" I ask.

"My dad's still old and drooling and my stepmother is still a gold digging 27-year-old."

"Same as always then."

"Oh yeah."

Kenzi is interesting cause she's hard to explain. Even with nearly 15 years of practice of trying to describe my best friend to people. I still find it almost impossible to explain her accurately. She's everything that doesn't go together. She lives to be different. Kenzi defies stigmas and stereotypes or at least tries to and sometimes she even defies all logic.

Kenzi the great I call her. In public with other people

she is painfully, painfully shy. You're lucky to get a murmur out of her if she doesn't pass out first. Yet that doesn't stop her from being herself and drawing attention to herself.

Since the beginning of time I always thought that shy people would dress conservatively and try to blend in. Do nothing to stick out that way they didn't have to socialize beyond their means. But Kenzi obviously never got that memo.

Her shy personality aside she maintains a grunge looks to offset her shyness. Blinding silver long wavy hair, a petite body structure, and clothing dedicated to her alternative grunge look like always. Which is great cause her clothes show her more outspoken side. But that doesn't necessarily help because she starts sweating and stammering like an idiot at the slightest compliment from a classmate or worst a complete stranger.

"So how was your weekend?" Kenzi asks me talking with her mouth full.

I want to tell her everything. Complain to her about

everything that's happened. I want to rant to her until the cows come home. But I just can't bring myself to do it. My hand clenches and unclenches as I try to make a decision to tell her. But my ultimate decision seems to be taking this one to my grave. Making this my first secret from my one and only best friend. Then again it seems like secrets have been a reoccurring theme in my life lately.

It's because of Menic. I know it. It's all his fault. If he hadn't made me feel like I was crazy for saying what I experienced I wouldn't be hesitant to share. Menic never rejects my ideals. All of a sudden with no one seemingly on my side including him I'm filled with self-doubt and hesitation. I wouldn't have anyone else to turn to. I don't know how I'd feel if I told Kenzi and she laughed at me or turned on me in some other way. I'm just not ready to risk it.

"Interesting in a boring way?" I say.

"What does that mean?"

"I was actually bored the entire break. I'm not use to things being so uneventful."

"Did you at least finish another masterpiece of yours?"

"Of course," I laugh "I said the break was boring. I didn't say I rolled over and died Kenzi."

"True." Kenzi replies.

"Hey, we have a test in math today, right?"

"Yep I'm so not prepared."

"To what luckily pass it like the straight a student you are?"

"Listen work and quizzes are boring and tedious especially when the answers are so obvious."

"There only obvious cause you are a mathematical genius unlike the rest of us who actually have to study."

"AP Calculus is a snooze fest. I don't want to take the test?"

"So, let's skip it." I say finishing my lunch which consists of last night's leftovers.

"What do you mean" Kenzi queries.

"Let's not take the test. Let's get out of here." I say in a nonchalant tone.

"You mean like skip class?"

"Yeah. I mean we're seniors and we've never skipped a class."

Kenzi puts the back of her hand against my forehead.

"Are you okay?"

"Yeah I'm fine why? I mean we don't have to if you don't want to."

"NO!" Kenzi says shocked "It's not that I don't want to I just never imagined you'd be the one pitching the idea."

"So where do you want to go?"

"Ya know we haven't went shopping together in a really long time."

"The mall it is then. I'll pack up and we'll head out when the final lunch bell rings."

"Man, today was a good day to get a parking spot up front then. Makes for an easier get away." Kenzi laughs.

"I'm taking that as a good thing because you never park up front."

We finish are lunches then take a quick trip to the bathroom. It's not long before the bell rings to end lunch and we use the rush of hallway traffic to make an escape. Although we almost got away no questions asked we get stopped by a female security guard.

"Stop right there."

Kenzi pulls me by the arm lightly to slow me to a stop.

"Where do you think you're going?"

"Um…" Kenzi stammers.

I slip the car keys out of her back pocket as the guard probably gives her an awkward look.

"What are your names?" says the lady with an unfamiliar voice.

"Ugh."

"She's Kenzi Parks and I'm Uvania Zhao." I say aloud.

"Who are you talking to? Look at me when you talk if you have something to say. By the way no glasses indoors."

"But miss-"

"It's okay Kenzi," I say, "I'll take off my glasses, but you won't like it?"

"School policy says no glasses."

"Okay but don't say I didn't warn you."

I remove my dark glasses from my face and just wait. I hold my glasses off to the side in my right hand.

"Oh my god what happened to your eyes. Their all white. You have no pupils!"

"Yeah, I know. I'm completely blind." I say as I wave my left hand in front my face theatrically.

"Oops I'm sorry. I just assumed-" the guard stammers.

"It's fine we were just heading out to Mr. Jamison's car to retrieve some teaching supplies for him as usual. Plus, you didn't know. It's not your fault." I show her the car keys as if they belong to the teacher.

"I'm sorry. Go ahead and continue." she then leaves probably feeling guilty and ashamed of herself for seemingly offending me. Though truthfully this is normal when I walk around in general, so it doesn't bother me all that much. I just wear the glasses, so people aren't forced to look at my all white eyes. I've been told it is very creepy.

Kenzi gets herself back together and manages to stop sweating. We exit the double doors of the school. In my eyes we are officially safe.

"Why did you give her are full names? What if she tells someone? What will we do?"

"Whose she gonna tell?" I ask "Mr. Jamison a teacher that doesn't exist. Plus, she's probably more focused on her offensiveness to a visually impaired student to share that story. So, don't worry."

"You seem quite confident about all this?"

"Trust me we have nothing to lose."

We arrive at Kenzi's green sedan and she helps me into the car, so I don't hit my head. She slams the door shut and then heads around to the driver's seat. She slides in and the car roars to life.

"So, what's are first stop?"

"Sephora." we say in unison.

We both laugh and make chit chat along the way.

Now we are alone in her car and I think now is a good time to tell her. My mouth disagrees though because no words are coming out. I'm starting to believe my tongue thinks explaining the entire situation is like reciting the worlds hardest tongue twister.

"We're here." Kenzi sings.
"Awesome!"

We both get out the car and we head to Sephora. Kenzi's dragging me along so fast that I can't even keep up. I stumble over my feet twice, but I find a way to manage. Kenzi doesn't even notice I'm sure.

When we walk through the sliding doors of the store and are greeted with cold air and the smell of cosmetics I want to pass away and take a vacation to heaven. Following my nose to the perfume section and the air growing colder around me I take notice that Kenzi is no longer nearby. I bet she wondered over to the eyeshadow section again.

Letting her absence leave my mind I let

myself fall into a paradise of aromas. Some smell purely of alcohol while others maintain sweetness. Every now and again I smell some that have been on the tester self that have sat here to long and separated and now just smell sour. I cringe at those and put them back full of regret of ever picking them up.

"Uvania." Kenzi whispers.

I turn my head in different directions trying to figure out which way the sounds coming from.

"Uvania down here." Kenzi says grabbing my shoulders and pushing me down in a crouched down position.

"Kenzi what happened? Why are we hiding?"

"Menic." she whispers.

"My brother?" I say confused "What about him?"

"He's here in the store?" she states, "Should we talk to him?"

"What is he doing?" I ask her.

"It looks like he's buying makeup. For a girl maybe?"

"He hasn't mentioned anything about girls to me lately."

I take a minute to think. Menic hasn't talked to me about much lately though. This would somewhat justify his new behaviors. Why a secret though. He knows better than anyone I wouldn't get involved in something unless he asked me to. So why the secret.

"So, a secret lover? Interesting."

"Doubt it but I don't know what else to make of it?"

"So, what's our next move girly?"

"Do not engage. Under any circumstances. None."

"Oh my god."

"What happened? What is it?"

"He's leaving."

"So?"

"With two bags worth of palettes and lipstick cases."

I tilt my head sideways thrown off by this new information.

"Where did he get the money?"

"That's a good question Kenzi. A good question

indeed."

"Alright well he's completely out of sight now so should we continue shopping."
"You know what I just remembered I actually have something I need to do. Ugh. . .do you mind taking me home."

"No not at all. Is everything alright Uvania."
"Sure. Perfect."

Kenzi and I make our way to the car and she drives me straight home. I thank her for the ride and head in my room. After explaining to my parents that I had totally forgotten that today was an early release day and Menic said he had somewhere to be, so I just had Kenzi drop me off. Despite my stammering from not being a good liar they buy into it anyway. At least I think they did.
I make my way to my safe haven and let out a deep breath. I don't know if I can take any more of this. Am I really just supposed to carry the world on my shoulders? Am I supposed to lose everyone close to me in the process.

Starting up on research again I pull out my phone, plug in my earphones, and begin my long journey of scowering the internet or, so I thought. I take everything I've learned so far and turned it into one gigantic google search. I type in "Astral travelling to my dream world where I have sight when I'm actually blind." At first, I thought it was way too long with too many key terms to actually bring up anything of use, but I was wrong.

There was one result, one link, just lingering. Staring at me providing some type of hope. If this link proved I was sane I'm going to show Menic straight away. It will be everything I need to clear my name. I would even be able to tell Kenzi about this discovery.

If it was wrong. If it was complete and utter garbage I'll probably curl up in a ball and accept that I've gone completely insane. I roll over the link and click it. My phone reads the information to me. The name of the website is This is not a dream. The page doesn't say much but it has four stories on it. It speaks of a secret society group called the Peira. It was like someone had typed up everything that I had experienced. From being blind to how it felt to see in a dream. But the one thing that still confuses me is that I still don't have enough information to know how to travel back to Athala. But the website was good enough to show my brother. He could read their stories and then everything would be fixed again. Well almost everything.

I hear the front door open and bags rustling about. Menic's home time to go rub it in. I wait for him to put the bags down and yell across the house. "Menic I need to talk to you."

Then I just make my way outside to the porch. After all it is my new favorite spot. Menic comes and sits next to me minutes later.
"I found it. I found evidence look at it." I say excitedly.

"Okay, okay calm down." he says.
He takes the phone from me. Everything is silent for a while. He must be in shock that there are other people out there with the same experience as me. If I

were him maybe I would be too. Actually, I am shocked. But I don't care because it means I'm not insane.

"Uvania." he sighs breaking the silence.
"Yeah."

"There's nothing here."
"You're lying there's an entire website right there."

"Uvania I'm telling you I don't see or hear anything I know how to use your phone. I'm sorry but there's nothing there."
He hands me back the phone and walks inside.

"Another thing. This is my last time telling you. Menic isn't my name."

<u>Chapter 8</u>

It's been hours since I've told Menic and I'm still blubbering like a new born baby. I know what I saw. I know what my phone read to me. Why is this happening? I'm starting to hate everything. My life, my family, anything and everything has just gone to hell. I thought bad things only happened to bad people. So why had this happened to me. What did I do to deserve this?

Maybe I just need a new plan. I need to actually find someone in Athala. The website proved other people have been there. So maybe I will find someone like me there. Then we can meet up in the real world. Then I won't be considered insane. My ideas become more and more far-fetched I realize this. It's still worth a shot though. I can't just let this go.

I haven't painted today! Did I even paint yesterday? Maybe I'm going insane but for a completely different reason. I quickly grab a blank canvas sketch out my famous pupil less eyes, a small butterfly, and quickly under paint them in watercolor. When it dries I climb back in bed and fall asleep as a tear strolls slowly down my cheek.

"Where am I?" I say "I know I'm in Athala, but this isn't the place I was before. It's scorching hot here."
"That depends where you were before. I don't know where that was, but this is East Ravic."
"East Ravic?" I repeat.

A man slowly appears in front of me as my eyes adjust. His hair is fine and brushed back into a mohawk. Sides shaved off of course. It's a silver color and oddly fitting for such a pale Asian guy. His skin is snowy and his eyes a solid green color that just kind of captures you making you never want to look away.

"Who are you?"

"My name is Pippy nice to meet you."

"Pippy." I say bamboozled if I heard correctly.

"I know. Not a common name but what can you do." he laughs.

"I've never seen anyone here before. What brings you here to such a desolated and sandy place." he asks.

"I don't really know. I was hoping to come back to the warm lake side sun beaming off your cheeks part of Athala but I'm here."

"Bryvile is where you were. Now your here. Hmph. Interesting." Pippy says.

"Anyway, I'm looking for someone. I'm looking for someone who is a part of a group called the Peira."

"I know them. I can tell you right now that you

definitely won't find any of them here. But I know where they are. Sadly, for some reason I can't get out of here. So, I can't take you to them."

"So, their definitely real." the words slip out of my mouth barely above a whisper.

"As real as you and me."

"Well I really need to find them so if you could take me to them I'd be forever grateful."

"I would if I could leave here. But I can't." he explains.

"Can't you just tell me where they are?" I press him for information.

"Travelling Athala isn't easy. Even if I drew a map you probably still wouldn't get to where you need to go. Not to mention travelling throughout Athala is different for everyone. Even the people of the Peira."

"Okay so if I help you get out of here; East Ravic. You would take me straight to them."

"Of course! If you helped me escape this forever scorching heat, I'd be forever indebted to you."

"If that's the case I'll help you. I really need to find them and you're the only person I've come across this far, so I don't have much of a choice."

"Alright but first things first. We have to figure out how you get here in the first place. By us I really mean you. Like I said before it's different for everybody."

"That's a broad statement. Where do I actually start?"

"Figure out how you got to Athala the first time around."

"Okay I'll try but how will I find you again?"

"I don't know. But something tells me we'll figure that out too."

"Well, I definitely hope your right."

The earth beneath us shakes and trembles. Wait no it's just me. Everything I'm seeing is shaking. Blurring. Pippy has become three separate images all mirroring each other. Why is everything losing color. Everything's turning white. Where's all the color going? Where is everything? I'm falling. I'm falling through nothing.

"Uvania!"

I gasp for breath clutching my chest hard. I feel cold beads of sweat dripping down my body. I calm myself and steady my heart beat. It took me a minute before I had completely stopped hyperventilating. That is something I never want to experience again.

"Uvania, what's up with you? You were sleeping harder than the dead. You stopped breathing for a minute. You almost gave me a heart attack."

"Well I'm not dead." I say to him.

"No thank you. Technically in a weird way I just saved your life."

"Thanks." I say as I throw the blankets off of myself.

"Did I do something wrong?" he asks genuinely.

"I don't know you tell me. You're the one who's been acting weird towards me. Actually, you've been acting weird in general."

"Uvania what are you talking about?"

"I saw you at the mall yesterday Menic. Kenzi

and I were at the mall and we saw you."

"Why would I be at the mall? I bought your present last week. I came to wake you up, so you could come eat breakfast and you could open your birthday present at the table?"

"My present." I say in wavering tone approaching him with caution "Menic what day is it?"

"It's your birthday hello. It's obviously December sixth."

"Menic."

"Uvania your being weird what is it?"

"Menic my birthday was almost a week ago. Today's the twelfth."

"You're so funny."

"Menic I'm serious." I say firmly.

I hand him my smartphone. He hesitates. Finally, I hear the screen unlock itself. He reads the date and freezes. He sucks in a quick breath in horror.

"What! That's impossible! People don't just forget an entire week like that do they?" he says.

76

He takes out his own smartphone and unlocks the screen reading the date to make sure were both not crazy. In the back of my mind I think he's also making sure it's not me pulling some cruel and twisted prank on him.

"How did I?"

"I don't know. Don't worry we will figure this out? We're not gonna tell anybody. Um I might tell Kenzi but that's different. Just pretend you've been here all week. Pretend like you didn't even forget six days."

"I'll try my best. I really hope we figure this out. Well I'm gonna eat. We're having pancakes by the way."

"Okay." I tell him.

Menic leaves the room and shuts the door behind him. I get ready and brush my hair. All I can find myself thinking is. My family life has gone to hell. I'm not even sure what's real and what's not. All I know is I'm finding more questions than answers. I start doing some research before I even think about leaving my room and following the sweet aroma of pancakes that probably has a jar of syrup next to it waiting just for me. It's just that I want to do a little research on how Menic's been acting lately. When he acts like that I tend to get really worried and quite annoyed. Though I wouldn't be surprised if Menic has lost his mind with everything that's going on.

Quick to unlock my phone I start typing in things like Why is my brother acting like two different people I'm getting worried? Results of all kinds come up. A lot of people will mention how their brother/spouse/husband acts like different people and how lovely they find it but it's not exactly what I'm looking for. I want answers not people's life stories. The internet can be helpful at times but those moments where it's being completely useless are the moments I want to scream till glass cracks or I lose my voice. Whichever comes first hopefully not the latter.

"Uvania get in here!" my dad screams angrily.

I raise an eyebrow in confusion. My dad's yelling at me. That's never happened before so I make my way to the kitchen having not gotten much accomplished, but it can wait for now. I take my seat at the table and everything feels kind of normal yet really weird.

"Yes" I say drawing out the s.
"Oh nothing, your food was getting cold that's all."

Oh, great my dad's acting bipolar now. Maybe normal wasn't the proper term cause the more time passes the more it dawns on me this family is anything but normal. If anything, normal is what is needed here. Which means straight after breakfast I'm telling Kenzi to meet me in the park.
"So how did everyone sleep?" my mom asked.

"Does it matter?" my dad responds.
"To me yes it does I want to make sure my family is taken care of."

"They slept fine."
"I didn't ask you. I asked the kids." my mom says angrily.

I lean towards Menic "You probably don't remember but they've been fighting for a while.

You've saved me from dealing with them so now it's my turn. Let's get out of here before we get caught in a cross fire."

"Oh okay," he says taking my word for it "I have quizzes I need to be studying for anyway. I guess I can head to the library."

"Alright if I figure out anything I'll either come and tell you or I'll call you. So please make sure your phones charged."

"I will."

My parents have turned a small question and to a volume war. Shots are being fired relentlessly and a lot of them seem below the belt. Especially for adults. They don't even recognize us. Menic and I literally just up and left this time. We didn't even try to hide it. They hate each other so much they don't even put effort in to hide it now. The world is a cruel place.

Arriving outside Menic doesn't even stop he kinda shouts a see ya later and keeps walking down the left lane. I take the right path and head to the park and send Kenzi a text saying I need her help with something. She asks is it about my brother due to recent events. I just said kinda.

While walking I kick little pebbles with my foot. Or at least the ones I can tell are in my way. At the park I don't hear anything. No kids, no wind, no cars. I go and play on a swing set pushing myself ever so lightly every now and again. Eventually Kenzi makes it.

"So, what's up buttercup? You said you had something to tell me?"

"Well," I start off "Menic's been acting like two different people. There's something off about him and I don't know what. Then this morning it got even more weird?"

"Weird how?" she asks.

"Well he didn't know what day it was?"

"I don't even know what day it is. I just know I don't have to go to school."

"No, Kenzi like he still thought it was my birthday. He genuinely doesn't remember like the past week. He totally freaked out when I told him. He didn't even remember . . ."

"Remember what?"

"Nothing, nothing. He just has been really strange."

"Well I'm almost positive that nothing is something but I can see you don't want to talk about it so I won't push." she tells me.

"I know how much you want to be a psychologist and stuff so I'm telling you this in confidence. We haven't even told my parents about this."

"You mean your parents didn't notice themselves?"

"They've been busy with work and stuff."

"Well your dad is a stockbroker. So, I could imagine that."

"Yeah, anyway I know it's not a lot to go on. I'll keep you updated. Lately I've really needed someone to talk to."

"Well I'm always here for you."

"I know."

THE REALM PAINTER

<u>Chapter 9</u>

It's been hours since Kenzi left. I'm sure it's dark outside too. Or at least sunset. I kick the sand beneath my feet backward and forward. I'm not really sure what I'm feeling or what I thought I would accomplish. It's strange. I used to feel so connected to everyone around me really. Now I feel completely alone. I've lost trust in people. It's not a good feeling really.

My phone vibrates in my lap like it's gone crazy. It turns out to be a text message from my mom. She says that dinner will be ready soon. I want to say that I'll be home soon. I want to say that I don't feel like eating. I want to say a lot of things to a lot of people. But I don't so I just reply ok.

I head home quickly so my mother doesn't begin to worry. Menic opens the door when I arrive. He asks me if I've learned anything. I tell him not yet and we both join my parents at the table for dinner. It's funny how Menic seems to be a lot more hesitant than I. But Menic is probably reluctant to be here for completely different reasons I'm sure.

This dinner is silent. No one even eats. It's like we were all broken or something. There were even moments where it seemed like we were all waiting on someone else to speak up. No one ever did though. We all just sat there at the table like a bunch of idiots. At one point my dad just gave up all together threw out the food and walked away. Menic and I took this as a means of escape to hang out in our new spot. Not all too soon though before Menic wasn't acting like Menic anymore.

"Well that was awkward." I start off.

"To say the least."

Menic's voice had changed to more of a bass note within seconds. A thousand things cross my mind within those milliseconds of time. I'm not sure exactly where to start with all my thoughts so I continue to just talk.

"So, I have to ask. What did it feel like this morning when I told you it wasn't my birthday? That it had been a week."

"What are you talking about? I saw you last night. I remember everything. No one could forget anything like the hell we've been through the past few days." he tells me.

Not what I expected him to say. But the way he now formed and structured his sentences was now becoming more and more familiar to me. Like it was becoming normal.

"So why did you lie then, Emmanuel?"

It felt awkward calling Menic by his first name. I hadn't called him that in what felt like the last decade. I can barely recall a single memory in our childhood when I called him by his legal name. I don't know. It just never seemed right back then. It's even more strange now.

His lip raised at the corner forming some type of sly smirk. I can tell because he lets out a small evil short laugh. What does he think this is an old movie? It's strange but I don't call him out on it.

"That's not my name." he tells me.

I want to scream at him. He never makes any sense. I mean if it's not his legal name and it's not his nickname. Then what could it possibly be. The heavens send me an answer. It's so simple. I wish I'd realized this sooner.

"So, Emmanuel isn't your name either?" I state.

"Nope."

"Are you even my brother?" I ask harshly in a confused tone.

"Yeah." he says smoothly.

I can tell his face is pointed toward the

ground now. I'm not sure if the smile is on his face still. I'm more focused on my questions and getting answers.

"So, if your name isn't Menic and it's not Emmanuel. What is it?" I ask facing the direction his voice came from.

He laughs at first before he gives me a straight answer.

"It took you long enough. I was beginning to think you'd never figure it out. All you had to do was ask?"

"So, what's your name? You still haven't told me." I say getting a bit irritated.

"Jasper," he tells me "My name is Jasper."

"Ok," I say "I'll call you Jasper. Unless mom and dad are around."

"Sounds like a plan." he agrees.

"Oh, and since you say you remember everything. Somehow. What's with the makeup haul? I saw you at the mall. Are you dating someone?"

He hesitates to answer. His breathing stops. He laughs a bit.

"No. I'm not dating anyone."

"So, what's with the make up?" I question again.

He claps his hands making a loud thunderous sound and rubs them together.

"Well this one. Sadly, I cannot tell you the answer to."

"Why not?" I say angrily.

"It's not my secret to tell."

The atmosphere from Jasper changes all of a sudden. It softens. It seems different. He seems different. What just happened. Why the sudden change?

"When did we get outside?" a lighter voice says.

"Menic?" I say.

"Yeah." he responds.

I look at him and kinda just stand there in disbelief.

"Did I do it again?" he asks me worried.

"Don't worry about it. I think I just got more information to tell Kenzi." I tell him in a sisterly tone.

"Seriously I can't believe I zoned. I hope we figure this out soon." he says.

"We will." I reassure him.

His stomach grumbles loudly.

"Foods on the table. It might be a little cold now though, so you might want to warm it up." I say in a sisterly and caring tone "Head in and eat. I'll be inside in a minute."

"Okay." he responds as he walks inside and shuts the door behind him.

"That bastard." I yell when I deem Menic out of ear shot.

Chapter 10

I start to paint A new sound in my room. I'm putting down the first oil painting layer. I try to focus on the accessories of the painting. They help tell the story but it's not really the subject per say. I focus on things like the wooden violin the girl is playing. Instead of painting cliché music notes I paint golden butterflies flying away. Not only are these things important to the painting but I've never painted them before, so I want to be careful and get it right. I can be lazy later.

After spending about 2 hours painting fine details in on the many different angled butterflies. Not to mention painting the wood of the violin and it's bow. Fun but it was also a nightmare. I'll do the background tomorrow. Right now, I want to get some sleep. I put the painting away for it to dry and flop into my bed. I pray that tomorrow is a good day then completely black out.

"This looks familiar and different?" I mumble.

"That's because we're in East Ravic. A different part this time. Nice to see you again. I was starting to think you were never coming back." says Pippy.

"I couldn't just not come back even if I wanted to. I don't know how much I miss the endless sand compared to Bryvile. But I definitely wanted to talk to you again. I told you I needed to find the Peira and that I was going to help you get out of here. I meant that." I state seriously.

"I see. Does that mean you've come back with new

information?" he questions.

"In a way." I say.

"In a way. That's code for that's a long story." he says to me.

I just stare at him.

"Let's gather some firewood then. It'll be dark here soon." he says walking into the woods.

"Where are we going to find wood in the desert?" I ask him.

"We're in the North of East Ravic. So, there are some fallen trees still. Since I seem to be the only one living here I've been rationing out the amount I use."

"Still confused." I interject "Trees and deserts don't grow in the same area."

"Right I never drew you a map. So Athala is a multi-leveled realm. Once upon time it was all just one massive chunk of land. But something similar to an earthquake happened. The different types of lands split up and separated pretty far too. It's like … a spiral staircase or a three-dimensional chess board. SO… when that happened some of the trees near Bryvile fell over on-"

"The North coast of East Ravic." I finish.

"Ding ding ding, correct." Pippy replies walking over hills of sand.

"Multi-level realm. No wonder you said you couldn't draw a map or help me get there on my own. Sounds complicated."

"It is. The lands spread out pretty vastly. Even if you stand on the edge and look out you'd see nothing. Up, down, or forward. Not a single sight of land. Therefore, making it impossible to even guess how far apart you'd have to travel. You know assuming teleportation is real. You can't just poof 400 feet over onto the next bit of land mass."

"I see."

"Which is why I'm still stuck here. But now I have you. So, let's hope the saying is true."

"What that 'two heads are better than one'." I say

"That's the one." he laughs.

We stumble upon his ration piled of twigs. Pippy is secretly part otter because it seems like he's organized and built a nice dam out of all the wood. There's stacks of bundles of what seems to be gray birch wood. He grabs two stacks and I manage to carry one. Pippy makes it look easy. He places the two side by side and says I can sit on one. He takes the stack from me and uses that one to make a fire. It's not long before I see smoke and a slowly growing fire. He comes and sits next to me.

"So, what do we know so far?" he asks me.

"I know that parts of Athala resembles my paintings at home. The first time I came to Athala was the night of my birthday when I made a wish to be able to see. I met you the night I started a new painting named Perspective. That's about it. I don't do much. I just oil paint all day. I don't think that's much to go on."

"You made a wish?" Pippy says in disbelief.

"Yeah my mom was being annoying. She always hesitates when she talks about my visual impairment. I just didn't want people to have to keep going through that when their around me."

"Ah, I understand better now." he says in a matter of fact tone.

"I don't know what made the wish actually work. It just did." I tell Pippy.

"You said your paintings look like Athala. Do any of them look like Bryvile?"

"Yeah actually. My painting rebirth looked like the lake in Bryvile." I tell him recalling that first night. "What about the others?"

"Well," I begin "The other painting called Perspective. It's a hybrid of a moth and a butterfly. I don't see how that would relate to Athala. I started a new painting recently called A new sound. It's a girl playing the violin with some more butterflies in it. It's in the early phases. There just artworks. Why?"

"I thought it was interesting. That's all. I don't know many artists."

"Enough about travelling to this realm and back. Let's talk about you. How did you get here? Where are you from?" I tell Pippy.

"I'm from Miami, Florida. I'm not sure how I got here. I mean I don't really remember. I remember meeting the Peira and getting to know them. They're so nice. I also remember waking up here one day and realizing I could never leave. It's fuzzy, my memory. I've been in this desert for years. I've had all the time in the world to think. I honestly can't remember much of my life before the Peira. There's not too much worth remembering after I saw them last." he tells me.

"That's really all you remember?" I say.

"Yeah."

"Well maybe when we find them you'll start to remember."

"That'd be nice honestly."

"Yep."

The ground began to shake. I was getting a bit dizzy.

"Uvania what's wrong?"

"I think I'm starting to wake up." I say in a panicky tone.

"Ok quickly. Put a list together of dates, time, location, and paintings."

<u>Chapter 11</u>

Screaming feels the house with terror what is happening? Jumping out of bed and grabbing my phone I run towards the sound. It seems to be coming from the bathroom.

"Emmanuel Zhao what are you doing!"

"What's happening dad?" I say.

"Your brother is wearing stuff on his face."

"Yeah. It's called makeup?"

"I don't see what the big deal is?" Menic continues in a feminine voice.

"Oh god. Janet come talk to your son!" my dad yells.

I just stand there in disbelief. I don't have anything against it. It's just not what I expected. I really did think maybe Kenzi was right. I thought the makeup was at least a gift for someone else. To find out now that my brother bought it for himself. I'm not sure what to say.

Menic continues to stand in the doorway in the bathroom. I push him in and lock the bathroom door behind me. I'm not sure what's going on, but I have a feeling it's better that I handle it before my mom even lays eyes on him.

"What are you doing?" he says to me. "Listen, I don't know what you're thinking by putting on makeup but you gotta take it off. At least for now. Your gonna give our parents a heart attack."

"They'll be fine. They'll get use to it." he assures me.

"Okay. Who are you? You're obviously not my brother and I'm pretty sure that make up isn't Jasper's thing. Not to mention you sound completely different."

"Well of course I sound different. I'm a girl. I've heard you been waiting to see me. So here I am. You found me." she laughs.

"Just tell me what your name is." I say in a desperate tone.

"Call me Carrie." she says.

"Well, Carrie. I wish I could say nice to finally meet you but the current circumstances doesn't make that sound so fitting."

"I see."

"Menic what's going on. Why is your father repeatedly saying that this family is falling apart? What happened?" my mom interrupts.

I hold my breath and my eyes dart to Carrie. I don't know her well enough. My mom doesn't know I'm in here. I hope Carrie plays her cards right. For all our sakes.

"Umm...it's nothing. I'll be out in a minute. Don't worry about it." Carrie states calmly.

"Fine." my mom says, "I have to make

breakfast anyways."

"Well she's gone now." Carrie points out.

"Carrie listen to me. You can't go out the house looking like that. You can't even leave the bathroom looking like that." I tell her.

"Does my makeup really look that bad?" she asks me.

I tilt my head to the side. Is she serious?

"Oh!" she says out loud "Jasper just informed me your blind. My bad."

"Yeah, I am. Honestly your make up probably looks great but it's just. How do I say this? Not appropriate for our family who can be traditional and very conservative."

"I see." she says in a sad voice "I'll take it off. I just wanted to express myself. It's hard being a girl in a guy's body. Plus, I rarely come out as it is. I guess I got overly excited. I'll clean up in here."

"An I'll buy you time out there. I'll make it up to you I promise."

"Okay I'm holding you to that."

By the time I get to the table my parents are

at some kind of a standoff. They've finished their breakfast from what I can tell. The foods aroma isn't in the air which means it's cold already.

"So, how's my son?"

"He's fine." I reply.

"He's broken there's no way he's fine."

"He's not broken." my mom says defensively.

"He's just trying something different. I'm sure it's just a phase. Don't worry." I say knowing that's what parents tend to think when in a hopeful manner.

"There's nothing wrong with exploring?" my mom adds.

"I hope your right about this Uvania." my dad says ignoring my mom's commentary.

"Good morning." Jasper says.

"Good morning Ja- I mean Menic."

"Thank god, your face isn't still covered in that stuff."

Mom and I shoot a glare at dad.

"I mean nice to see your ready for a new day."

Which isn't really better or makes any sense. But he's already made the atmosphere awkward, so I guess there's no coming back from that is there.

"You know what I think I'll just head to work." my dad says.

"I have laundry to fold." my mom follows up.

Maybe there's hope for us yet. My phone jumps around in my pocket. I receive a text from Kenzi.

Jasper reads out loud over my shoulder "I got some information for you. Meet me at the park ASAP."

"Shall we?" Jasper says.

"Yeah, maybe we can finally get an understanding of what's going on with you and Carrie. Hopefully I can find out how to get my brother back."

<u>Chapter 12</u>

Jasper and I arrive at the park together. He informs me that Kenzi is sitting at the bottom on one of the 2 lane slide. Before we go up to her I remind Jasper that they've never met before. So, if possible to act more like my real brother. Jasper assures me that he'll at least try.

We walk over to Kenzi. Jasper helps me sit beside her. I'm not sure what to expect. Should I say something? But what would I say to her. She invited me out here after all.

"Uvania," she whispers interrupting my thoughts "Why'd you bring Menic?"

"Well it's about him isn't it? He should be here. Plus, you can explain it better than I can. He might as well hear it the first time around right." "I guess. I just hope he's ready to hear it." she states.

"I can handle it." Jasper says making his presence known.

It then dawns on me that Menic isn't the one listening right now. It's all Jasper and he is definitely less emotional. I wouldn't be surprised if it didn't faze him. Maybe having Jasper around is a good thing after all. Let's just hope Menic doesn't suddenly come back out of nowhere during conversation.

"If you say so." Kenzi says.

"I'm ready when you are." I say.

"My psychology professor and I both thought of the same thing automatically really."

"Wait!" I interrupt "I forgot to mention the latest incidents that occurred."

"Oh, what are they." she questions.

"Well this morning I found him putting make up on his face. He called himself Carrie. Then there was this other time he called himself Jasper. I was all like where are these names coming from," I explain to her "Not to mention any name he goes by other than Menic he acts nothing like himself. It's just so random."

"Don't tell her I was putting make up on my face!" Jasper yells "That's embarrassing."

"It's ok. I won't tell anyone." Kenzi giggles.

"Alright, alright. Let's get serious. What did you want to tell us?"

"He's pushier than the last time we met." she points out "Anyway your right. So, when I told her what you said we both came to the same conclusion. At first, I wasn't ready to tell you but everything you just said more or less confirms it. Especially the makeup part."

"Really?"

"Yep, it's an uncommon disorder. And personally,

one of my favorites because it's very peculiar. It's called Dissociative Identity Disorder. Also known as Multiple Personality Disorder. DID or MPD for short."

"Multiple personality disorder." I repeat.

"Yeah. Imagine. You, me, and your brother sharing the same body. One physical body but three different mind sets. Three people with different personalities. Different habits, backgrounds, morals -"

"Genders." I interrupt.

"Exactly."

"You make it sound like I've lost my mind." Jasper says.

"I wouldn't say so. That has a negative connotation to it. I'd say it's expanded. It's not normal that's for sure. But if it's managed properly I don't think it's insane at all."

"Wait a second. Back up. What causes something like this. It sounds like a mental break down."

Kenzi laughs lightheartedly at my question "Come

on Uvania. What causes any disorder. Stress and some form of traumatization. Paired with an inability to cope."

"Trauma."

"I already told you what the trauma was." Jasper says.

"Yeah, I remember."

"So yeah. When the trauma happens with no ability to cope. In your brothers case it created different personalities. So, one of them could deal with it."

"Where's my brother then?" I ask her.

"He's there. He's not gonna disappear. He's the host. Just expect him to keep changing and not acting like himself. There's no cure really. But therapy is always recommended."

"Oh no. Now you're pushing it. No way."

"I thought you were pro psychologist."

I completely face palm at this. Kenzi's smart but sometimes she misses the obvious.

"Kenzi meet Jasper. Jasper this is Kenzi."

"Oh my god. I get to see an alter already. This is so cool."

I can imagine a sparkle in her eye at this moment. It's not soon after that I hear dirt sliding backwards under Jasper's foot. If I'm right Kenzi probably tackle hugged him at the thought of meeting an alter.

"Uvania...help. She's touching me. I don't like people touching me."

"Kenzi you heard him. Lay off."

"Sorry." she says in a childlike voice "I got really excited."

"I can see that. Well we got the diagnosis let's go sis."

"What! No, you can't go I have questions. Questions I could only ask an alter."

"First off, I know you're excited and all, but would you stop calling me an alter. I'm still a person. I have feelings." Jasper tells her.

"Ok. Just a few questions I swear." she says to him in a hopeful tone.

"Fine. A few. That's it."

"How many personalities are in your system?"

"System?" Jasper says sounding confused.

"Yes, it's called a system."

"Well its Menic, Carrie, and me." he says hesitantly.

"That's so awesome." she says.

"Can you talk to the other alters?"

"Yeah?"

"Kenzi calm down. I can tell your scaring my big brother." I state.

"Big brother?" they say in unison.

"Well you might as well be." I state.

"I'm confused." Jasper states.

"As am I." Kenzi follows up.

"Sorry I just. You seem like a big brother to me. Your even more honest than Menic and frankly more blunt. The things you say don't always make sense at the time. But it's usually in my best interest." I explain.

"When you put it that way-"

"Wow he does sound like a big brother?" Kenzi says starry eyed.

"Is she always like this?"

"Short answer, yes." I laugh.

"And the long answer?" he queries.

"Only to her living breathing psych patients."

"I'm not a patient." he says defensive.

"That's not gonna keep her from analyzing you and making a mental profile."

"ok..." he trails off in a worrisome tone.

"Don't worry she won't bite."

"Can I get that in writing?" Jasper asks.

"Maybe another time." I laugh.

"So, what do we do now? Where do we go from here with this new-found knowledge? I mean are we gonna tell mom and dad now?"

"Maybe, but not today." I say.

"Remember this isn't an official diagnosis." Kenzi intervenes.

"Well it's all we have to go on. So, it is what it is."

"She's right." Jasper agrees.

My phone vibrates in my pocket. Menic tells me it's a text from mom. Apparently, she wants us home but didn't give a reason. We didn't question it with how things have been going lately so we just left on that note after giving Kenzi a goodbye hug.

<u>Chapter 13</u>

It's late and I can't sleep. Menic's out like a light so I can't talk to him as a distraction from this cursed insomnia. Not to mention the arguing my parents are doing. I wonder if their like this because it's more appropriate to get it all out when we're asleep. When we can't hear them. I wonder if this is their first fight? I mean at the table it's been a war no doubt, but they try to restrain themselves. This late hour fight is relentless war.

"John, how could you? You slept with

another woman. In our bed!" my mom yells.

"Lower your voice." my dad threatens.

"Have you no respect. No shame." she points out.

"It's not like you're ever interested." he shoots back.

"You're missing the point. I trusted you. You said never again. Was it not enough when I walked in on you the first time two years ago?" she screams.

"Apparently not. I don't know what you want from me Janet. I don't have some grand explanation for this. It just happened."

"But this didn't just happen. For crying out loud John our child walked in on you."

"He'll be fine."

"Ugh. Do you not understand the term consequences." she exclaims?

"Of course, I do. I'm a grown man."

"No, you're not. You're a bast-"

A sound echoes through the halls. It couldn't be. My dad...he'd never lay a hand on her. Not even if he was furious.

"Watch your mouth." he says in a stern voice. That's the last thing I hear. I wish I'd never heard it at all. Any of it. I'm too scared to say anything to them. Too scared to run inside and break it up before my dad did the worst thing possible.

I had hoped to tell them about Menic's condition by the end of the week, but I don't think I'm in the position to do so right now. Not just because I'm laid up in bed curled up in a ball hiding under the blankets either. At least Menic's asleep. That's the upside to all of this. What you don't know can't hurt you. Or in this case him.

<u>Chapter 14</u>

There was no breakfast when we woke up. Just my parents side by side at the table. Will this peculiarity never end?

"Sit down. We have something to tell you." my dad urges.

"It's not easy either. We spent a lot of time talking this over." my mom says.

"What's going on?" says Jasper.

"We are getting a divorce." my mom states.

"When?" I say.

"Well me and your father agreed on this decision, so we'd figured we'd go down to the office and file the paper work after telling you two."

Jasper says hesitantly "Is that your way of sugar coating today. Like you guys are leaving right now."

"You are. Aren't you. You're leaving now that's why there's no breakfast!"

They start making their way to the door. I hear a series of fumbling keys as I stand still in disbelief.

"Bagels are in the fridge." she calls out.

"Bagels?" says Jasper.

"Was that as weird to you as it was to me?" I ask.

"Without a doubt." he says.

"I'm super confused and conflicted so I'm going to go paint in my room and then take a nap. When I wake up this will all just be a bad dream or something." I say.

"Okay, whatever you say. I'll be walking around town looking for something to keep my mind occupied." he says.

Jasper heads out and I head to my room. I quickly find myself engulfed in painting the background with reds, browns, and even oranges. Three colors I hate but I'm going to use to create an appropriate background. At first, I was going to do something filled with trees and plenty of forest. Now I think I'm firm on the idea of making it more backyard like with mountains really far out into the distance. Barely visible but there. I obviously use deep greens for tree leaves. Blues and grays for the snowy mountains.

I find myself quickly tiring and fingers cramping. I must be a bit out of practice. Either way I have earned a well-deserved break from all the progress I made. I completed the entire background after all. Alright time for a nap I tell myself.

◊   ◊   ◊

"Oh, great. Now, where am I?" I say practically screaming

in frustration.

"We're in West Ravic."

"But how. You're not able to leave East Ravic, right. That's what you told me." I say.

"You must have done something right." he says.

"Well I did but I don't know what. Not to mention we still haven't found the Peira."

"Patience." he says.

"I know."

"So, what have you painted lately?"

I tell him every detail of my new painting. Hoping we can find the tiniest clue to why. That way this can all be over. I think it's about time that someone cracked the code to solving the puzzle. If we don't find the Peira soon I'm honestly calling a quits.

"You have to wake up. Paint a picture of the mountains. No other landscape included. Just the mountains. From what I'm guessing in all your paintings. You didn't meet me until you started painting the butterflies. I'm not sure how I feel about that. But make sure you paint one of those as well. Also stick to your *signature as usual and paint the eyes pupil less. I believe*

that's how you've been sending yourself here. To Athala. It

has to be. Nothing else makes sense." Pippy says.

"*I'll try it when I wake up." I tell him.*

"*No, wake up now!" he says.*

I don't respond.

"*Wake up! Wake up!" he repeats.*

"Hello! Hello!" I hear Kenzi beating on the door

frantically.

"Hello. It's the police."

"Uvania, I know you're in there. Please open the

door."

"Coming!" I yell back "Just a second."

I grab my things and rush to the door. I swing it

open in one giant motion. What's happening?

What's wrong? Kenzi was so loud and panicky.

Something happened. If the police are here. Well it's

even worse.

"Hey." I say casually "What's the matter?" I say sounding slightly more concerned than I wanted to lead on.

"Well -" the police officer starts.

"Wait!" Kenzi interrupts "Where's Menic?"

"We don't have all day!" the cop on the right says roughly.

"This is important! Unless you want to have to explain this twice I'd be more patient!" Kenzi yells at him.

"Fine, we'll wait."

"I'm sure it's hot outside. Come in so you're not just standing there in the heat," I say as I let them in "I'll get you some drinks."

"That would be lovely." the other officer says.

I run to the kitchen to make a big pitcher of lemonade. I take it to the living room and go back to the kitchen for cups of ice. Then I text Menic to come home and tell him that it's an emergency. About 10 minutes later he bursts through the door and a truck outside takes off.

121

"What happened? Uvania are you okay? I got your message." says Menic.

"I'm fine. We waited. So, I'm still not a hundred percent sure why there here."

"Now that the brother is here. We can finally move on, go ahead and proceed."

"We came to ask you when you last saw your parents." the irritated cop says.

"This morning," Jasper says "Though it was odd because they dropped a bomb on us. Saying they went to the office to file for divorce."

"mmmm," the nicer cop groans uneasily.

"Why?" I say.

"You guys-" Kenzi starts "Your parents died in a car crash?"

"What happened?" I say, "explain it."

"A car crashed into them and they died on impact." the irritated cop says.

"It was quick. They didn't feel anything." says the nice cop.

The mean cop explains "They were crossing in a 4-

way intersection and a car sped ahead and bam. Car crash."

"Okay well who was the driver?" Jasper says. It gets quiet. Everyone is still. The atmosphere becomes eerie and thick. Did we say something unusual?

"Uh." Kenzi stammers.

"It was me," the irritated cop states "We got a call. I was driving. I turned on the lights then went full force ahead. Your parents we're in the middle of the street when crossing. There was nothing I could do." he says uncaringly.

"There was nothing you could do?" I say getting a bit angry.

"Nothing." he says.

"You killed my parents and you come here to tell me there was nothing you could do. You killed them!" I scream at the cop.

Jasper and Kenzi jump in front of me to hold me back and being too confrontational with the cop.

"You didn't even say you're sorry! You came

here to tell me what happened. Because of something you caused. You don't even sound like you care. You don't even sound like you're sorry in the slightest!" I scream louder.

"Look at me. NO! Look at me." Jasper says wrapping his hand along my jaw. Forcing me to look at him.

"They killed our parents!" I say screaming angrily and a bit sad.

"It's okay. It's okay. It'll be fine."

Jasper wraps his arms around me. He hugs me. Like I said before he's my big brother. A different part of my brother. But he's my brother. He's a good one too. My heart beat slows. I exhale slowly.

"It's gonna be okay. We have each other." he says as he lets me go.

"Get out of my house." I say at the cops sternly.

"Uvania." Kenzi says worried.

"We can't just leave. You two aren't adults. Uvania you're only 17 and Menic is only around 14 or 15. You have to-"

"Thanks for stopping by," I say "We can take care of ourselves. I am more than capable of taking care of my younger brother and managing our current household and its bills. We don't need any social worker or adoption services."

"Uvania." Kenzi says "There the police for crying out loud. You can't kick them out."

"Please leave and don't come back." I say opening the door.

The police man stands in the door "We'll have to come back. You realize that."

"I expected it to go a bit smoother." says the other officer under his breath.

"Have a nice day," I say "Also, if the police department wanted this to go smoother they wouldn't have sent the officer and his partner who killed my parents. Now as you know. I have a funeral to plan."

They both step out.

Kenzi says "Well you know where you can

find me. Call me if you need anything."

As she walks away I over hear more of the cops chatter.

"Well what do you want me to do. Handcuff her and drag her off the property." the nice one states.

"I guess not."

"She's right though."

"About what ?!" he says angrily and shocked.

"You could at least say sorry or sound remorseful."

"They don't pay me enough."

Chapter 15

"Do you realize what you just did Uvania. I mean where were you even going with that? Do you have a plan for when they come back?"

"Maybe, I'm not there yet. All I know is that we need to prove that we can support ourselves by the time they do come back. Or a way to stall. Something."

"Do you hear yourself?"

"I use to sell art. I made pretty good money off of it then. I'm sure I could pick back up on it."

"You sound insane," he tells me "You realize that right?"

"No, it could work. It could. So that's a problem solved."

"What problem solved? There is no problem solved. Those cops are gonna be back. Maybe with more cops. But definitely with CPS."

"I need to talk to Pippy."

"Whose Pippy?" he says trying to understand my mindless babble.

"I'm going to talk to Pippy. I'm gonna take a nap so don't wake me up." I say as I turn away.

"NO!" Jasper says grabbing me by the wrist "I may be a part of your brother. But I can't *be* your brother."

"I don't understand."

"Uvania, I can't keep taking all the hits for him. I was created to protect him. To help him cope. I know this. But Menic has to live his life too. I need you to have it together. Right now, Menic doesn't even have the slightest clue that our parents are dead. Do you get that. When I'm not in control any more you're going to have to explain it. Do you understand that? Are you ready for that?"

"I...guess."

"I need you to know. Because the minute I'm out of control I don't plan on coming back for a while. I understand that he needs to mourn. He needs this. I don't want to get in the way. It means that if it takes him months you won't see me for a long while. If I'm not here I can't protect you either."

"I... see."

"I need you both to understand that."

"I get it. Now let me go I need to see Pippy. I have to go! He's waiting for me in Athala."

"Is this about that dream place again. Uvania let it go. It's not real." he states angrily.

"Yes, it is. Listen my parents argued and bickered since I brought that place up. I have spent this entire time trying to clear my name. Now there dead. I'm not going to quit now. I practically caused my parents entire divorce. My dad cheating and stuff I'm guessing that was just the last straw. But I lit the match and added fuel to the fire."

"Uvania they're dead. Consider your name cleared. Let it go already."

"Even without the death of my parents. Clearing my name. The Peira are still society of people. Not just any people either. They're like me. I'm not going to let it go till I find them and see them face to face."

"Your gonna do this no matter what aren't you." he says.

"Yep, like it or not I'm going to Athala. I don't care if you don't think it's real."

He moans in muffled aggravation. I storm off to my room ready to test what Pippy said. I have to draw those mountains. They don't even have to be super detailed. I just need to start a new painting and be done with it.

But...what do I paint? I know what Pippy told me to paint but I'm not really sure I can't just paint that like some type of list. I still want it to look beautiful and artistic. It still needs to be a work of art. Think Uvania think. You can do this. Butterfly, Mountains, and pupil less eyes. Think.

Okay so you can start with the foreground. I'll make a bigger version of the mountains in my other piece where it was so tiny you could hardly see. So, it'll mostly be some blue tinted light gray mountains through most of it. Now that I know it's a landscape view maybe I should start with turning the canvas sideways. Okay that's better.

If I do it right I can totally put really huge eyes in the background of the painting. Those will replace the clouds. In theory everything's already coming together nicely. Or so it seems. It might be a whole different piece when I put brush to canvas. No, have a little faith I tell myself. You can totally do this. It needs color. It needs light.

Oh! I know. I can have red, blue, and orange colors creeping up the sides of the mountain. Like a nice sunrise to add some beautiful soft colors. Also, a gold butterfly. However, it's color nonetheless.

I start to attack the canvas with my brush

and paint like my life depended on it. Everything else was gone in my life. There was no sense of normality. So maybe my life did depend on it. My entire being. My whole identity did depend on this one piece. This one canvas I needed so badly. It needed to be more that art. It needed to be the portrayal of Athala, so I go to the right place. It needs to be eye catching. If possible as close to the Peira as possible.

I decide that it's quite rough around the edges. I realize I'm going to need to overhaul on fixing the structure and even out the paint. But it carries my concept and idea across. It also means that I'm opening an entire new chapter in my life and just go forward from here.

<u>Chapter 16</u>

"Pippy!" I shout.

"Here I am," he says to me "and there you are."
he says in a weird voice.

"Okay we're off of East Ravic." I state.

"Yes, now we are in Asylo."

"Asylo. More like Asylum."

"Well you did practically go insane to get here did
you not?" he retorts.

"Fair enough," I reply "Enough jokes though. Let's get a
move on."

"Sadly, this is where our journey together ends. We must go our separate ways. We've both held up our ends of the bargain."

"What do you mean?" I state angrily.

"I got you onto the correct plane within Athala. You got me off of that terrible, lonely, deserted island."

"So now I'm off to enjoy the frozen tundra and you are off to find the Peira. You no longer require my assistance." he says happily.

I shift my feet around in the two-foot snow. That's it he's just gonna leave me out here. How am I supposed to find the Peira on my own? I'm not even sure what I'm looking for. How would I know if I was closer to finding them or not? Where is he going? What's his hurry? Why is everyone abandoning me?

Pippy walks away leaving no tracks behind. Somehow, he's managing to not sink into the white blanket. He's only a few steps away when I finally get the nerves to speak up.

"Stop." I whisper.

Pippy continues to walk away. I'm not even sure he heard me.

"Stop it." I say a bit louder.

Still no reaction.

If he leaves me, I'll die out here. Alone and afraid with only mountains surrounding me. Asylo begins to feel like the nightmare you can't wake up from. The dream you just can't manage to shake even when you're awake. The one that haunts you. The rainy cloud over your head. I have to stop him.

"Stop!" I scream at the top of my lungs.

The ground beneath us starts to shake. The mountains, Pippy, everything starts to blur. It's shaking from left to right. I can't stand. I'm falling. Oh no, I've caused an avalanche. The snow is coming to murder us. I can see it coming down the mountain to the right of us. We're doomed. No wait out. We are both going to die, and our cause of death will be snowballs.

"Hello"

"She's waking up"

Voices. I hear voices of strangers. A teenage girl maybe. Are they talking about me? Where am I? I sit up straight. Then open my eyes. Automatically clenching my head from the pain of sitting up too fast and maybe something else.

"Whoa, whoa, whoa. Easy there. You really hurt yourself." an old man with gray hair says as he looks at me worriedly with pupil less eyes. I see him in the corner of my peripheral vision.

"What's your name?" the girl with a slightly pixie pitched voice asks me.

"Umm... my name... is Uvania." I say slightly dazed.

"Uvania is it. Well Uvania, what are you doing here?" she says.

"Where is here?"

"I'll ask the questions here." she says.

"No, I will," the old man says "I told you before. We don't bully answers out of people."

"Fine. Time has passed but not all has been forgotten." she says.

"So, what has brought you here to Asylo?" he asks

136

me.

"I'm here to find the Peira." I say blinking a few times to adjust my vision and then look directly at the girl.

"Holy mother of Asylo?!?!" she screams.

"Lilian, language." he says to her.

"But elder she has the mark. Her eyes." she tells him.

He stands up and looks at me. He stares intensely into my eyes. Leaning over carefully using his wooden cane for support. I don't say anything. I just wait for an explanation.

"Indeed, she does. How peculiar?" he says.

"I'd ask her friend or foe. But she's obviously a member of the Peira. The Peira has no foe." he says in a calm matter.

"Elder I think you are forgetting the incident."

"I haven't forgotten anyone. The Peira has no foe. The person you speak of is a fool."

"If you say so," the girl says a tad aggravated "Anyway back to you girlie. What do you remember? What was the last thing that happened?"

"The last thing that happened. I remember I was

screaming."

"At what a mountain? The Peira own this place. No one else is here but us." she says.

"I'm here and you didn't know about me." I say to her.

"This is true." the old man agrees.

"I wasn't yelling at a mountain either."

The old man wipes my arm clean of red snow. He bandages my bleeding arm soon after. Wrapping it tightly but leaving room for me to move my right arm with some comfort.

"I was yelling at a guy; his name is Pippy." I say to her.

The old man drops the bandage wrap and it rolls onto the floor leaving a trail.

"Idiot!" she screams at me.

The old man gathers up the bandage and rolls it back up.

"Why would you bring him back here! How stupid can you be? We left him abandoned for a reason."

"Lilian! That's enough." the old man states sternly towards her.

"No," she says, "It'll be enough when we kill him."

The girl with the pixie voice and died pink ends leaves the cave. Leaving the two flaps made of sheets of straw swaying back and forth. It was in that moment I realized that I had did something so terrible it was pass my own comprehension. And in this moment of feeling absolutely lost. I looked at the man she called elder.

"Don't worry. I'll explain."

<u>Chapter 17</u>

"I suppose *it started a long time ago,*" the elder began *"We found the first wanderer. What did you say his name was again?*" in an old-timers' voice.

"*Pippy.*" I said.

"So, Lilian had stumbled upon Pippy, the wanderer, and we took him in. We found him out on one of the parts just walking around. No idea how he got here. He didn't know. We didn't know so we took care of him. With no way of knowing how he specifically got here no way to send him back. He stayed. We taught him and showed him everything. How to survive. What we were capable of. We treated him like family."

"Awe, that sounds so sweet." I tell him.
"It was. Everyone loved him. We were all so close. If anyone had a secret. Pippy knew it. We all trusted him like a brother. Though to me he was more of a son." he cracks a smile with a sparkle in his eye while picturing the past.

"If he was like a son how do you forget his name" I giggle.
"I'm old. Give an elder a break. Like I said he was more of a son. My nickname for him was Wanderer. He never could sit still. Even after he was well adjusted with us here." he told me.

"I'm sorry. Pippy is my age. He's like 20. When you talk about him you make him sound like he's 5 or something. Are you sure we are talking about the same person?"
"Without a doubt." he responded "I'm just really old. He was so young. After all, do you know how old I am?"

"No."

"Exactly. Now back to the story." he tells me "Being so

young and what not he had to make friends with someone. That someone was Lilian. At the time they were the only one's here who were in the same age range. So, they would run away and explore together. Go swimming and do all the other things you young folks do."

"So, they were close? Then why does Lilian look like she hates him so much? What changed."

"He knew too much. He knew everything in fact. We found out that he was sharing our location with others who also where not of our kind. Telling them about all of Athala and the people who lived here." he said getting kinda sad and heartbroken "He made us sound like fools. He told them how to get here. He threatened the well-being of our very own safe haven. Apparently, he had even brought people here sometimes. Though there's no proof in this part. But there was a rumor he brought strangers here to see us and took them back. We were on display. Like freaks. Like animals."

"I'm so sorry." I whisper empathetically.

"But to Lilian it wasn't about the display in itself. She was more distraught about him posting our location on the

internet with the instructions. All our secrets. Every single member of the Peira Clan came here by a means to get away. In the outside world we were shamed for being different. For our eyes. For not fitting in. This is our safe place. Pippy invited strangers here with an all access pass. Our peaceful lives would be changed. This world would be like it was out there. The mocking and the laughing." he exclaimed.

"Yeah, I know what you mean." I say exhaling "The other side is quite something."

"Simply put he was foolish."

"Does anyone know what drove him to do such things of betrayal?" I questioned "Did you ever ask before you guys stuck him in that hot desert?"

"Nope, never got the chance to ask. Soon as Lilian told us, though without proof, his fate was sealed. No questions asked. Though it definitely had been him who'd done it."

"It's not exactly what I'd call a fair trial." I say.

"Me neither." he chuckles "but my daughter was so sure it was him. she was easily able to convince everyone else including the other elders that he had to be dealt with *immediately." he finished flatly.*

"I'm guessing she's not your daughter by blood than either." I state.

"You catch on quick." he laughs.

My sight starts fading in an out again. I'm not able to take it. I'm not resisting the fact that I know I'm about to wake up in my room. However, no matter how many times I go through this the nausea comes out of nowhere randomly. I can never prepare myself. Though I was here a long time compared to pass visits. I fall back asleep on the table I woke up on.

"Uvania!" my brother shakes me wildly back and forth.

"What huh? Who are you?" I say sleepy.

"Ha-ha very funny. You should recognize your own brother you know. Or at least my voice." Menic says to me.

"Ouch." I say.

"What happened are you hurt?" Menic starts to panic.

I look at my right arm to find a really big blue and purple bruise decorating my arm. I must have moved it the wrong way.

"Huh" I sigh "It's mostly healed. Still hurts though."

"What?"

"Don't ask long story."

"So, where's – my reward?" Menic's voice changes mid-sentence.

"ugh..." I snap my finger repeatedly "Oh! Carrie is that you."

"Duh who else?" she says bluntly.

Not gonna lie between her and the boys she's my least favorite person I like dealing with. Even after what happened earlier with Jasper.

"Hello, earth to big sister. We had a deal." she points out.

"Yeah I know. I'm working on it."

"Well work faster, I'd like to be able to express myself as a female sometime this month."

she says.

"Ok, ok. But you know it's Menic's body. Ultimately, it's up to him. I make no decisions. I'd only enforce what he allows." I explain "Now move out the way I need to talk to my brother."

"Whoa, I blacked out again." Menic says "It feels weird when I come back."

"Thank you for that interesting tidbit about your Multiple Personality Disorder." I say a bit weirded out by his comment.

"Sorry."

"It's fine. Hey how do you feel about a more androgynous look?" I ask him while carrying some of my art folders to my dad's office room.

His feet stop at the door. They make a squeaky sound. Though in Menic's case I assume it's due to fear. He hesitates. He doesn't have the best memories in here to say the least. Dad always side bar him into this room. Though I say other than that 90% of the time we were told to stay out of here.

Back when I first started selling my art he

use to just make me put my artwork in a folder and leave it by the door. He said that was my scan for later pile. Though well into that process he just finally let me in because he was too tired to do so. He simply couldn't keep up.

"Come inside. You're with me don't worry." I say.

"Yeah" he says.

The last time Menic was in this room had to be like 5 or more years ago. I know dad yelled at him. Really loud. I also remember Menic crying. I don't remember if he ever told me about what though. No point in asking now.

"So how do you feel?" I ask.

"About?"

"The androgynous look." I repeat.

"Oh, well be more specific. How androgynous are we talking?" he says raising an eyebrow.

"Well Carrie already tried putting make up on her face. She practically gave you away. Dad almost had a heart attack. Mom seemed pretty chill though surprisingly enough." I say trailing off as I log in and prepare the scanner. My dad never did use a unpredictable password.

"She did what?!" he yells.

"I'm blind not deaf." I state "However, I was thinking more along the lines of something a bit smaller for now. I was thinking maybe she could dye your hair."

"That sounds kind of reasonable." he says unsurely "But none of the hot pinks or neon colors."

"Of course not. I care about my little brother. I was thinking more of an auburn color."

"I guess that would be okay. Yeah I'd let her do that."

"You're very accepting of these personalities."

"That's because I think it's cool and interesting."

"Yeah if we can keep Carrie in check I don't think we should have that many problems." I say to him.

"True." Menic turns to the door "Can we leave? You scanned like 10 art pieces. I want to get out of here before dad comes home."

That's when I realize. I have to tell him. I have to tell him now. There's no way I can put this off till later. Plus, I'm sure quite a few people know already I don't want him hearing it from anyone else. Though I'm starting to think back to what Jasper and I discussed. I had to be ready. More importantly I looked him dead in the eye and said that I was.

"Menic..." I begin "Dad isn't coming home."

"What why? A business trip out of nowhere. Did he ditch mom right after signing the divorce papers? Where is mom anyway? Did she say where they were at?"

"Menic," I say calmly "Mom and dad never made it to the divorce office place. They died on the way there."

"What?" he says starting to cry a bit "Mom's dead? How?"

"It was a car accident. They were hit by a drunk driver."

"But mom's mom. She can't be dead." he says.

"Everyone died. Both vehicles. I'm sorry."

"No this can't be."

It seems that he just stood frozen in shock for a few minutes then decides to sit on the floor. I'd wrapped my arms around him and comfort him. But growing up together I can sense when my brother just needs time to heal. Right now, is one of those times.

I do feel bad though. I told him our parents were dead. I told him it was a drunk driver. I lied. Or to sugar coat it I stretched the truth. Menic's a good kid but when he's upset he can become irrational a bit. It doesn't happen a lot. But I'm afraid if I told him a cop did it. Well he'd try to kill the cop. Like I almost did.

<u>Chapter 18</u>

There's is so many things that have happened. So many things that have changed. So many decisions that need to be made and things to take care of. More than the average person. At least in my eyes. Honestly, I want to stay in Athala to avoid all the real-world problems. However, I don't want to abandon my brother. Leave here to mourn both our parent's death. Worst if I leave he will without a doubt get taken in by the government.

This is a lose-lose situation if I've ever seen

one honestly. I just have two worlds in my life. Both holding their own set of problems. I'm not good at making choices by any means. These two worlds are my 50-50 choice. If I choose between two worlds. There's a 50% chance that I make the best decision of my life. On the other hand, I have a 50% chance of ruining my life. I don't want to choose. But I can only handle one thing at a time. Though it's my life it does affect others. That's what I need to take in to consideration.

Why is no one here to help me? Why is it just me? Why is it all resting on my shoulders? This could've happened to anyone else, yet the cruel world chose me.

"Menic," I scream "Are you home?"
In response I get cold air filled with silence. Taking that as a no. How long was I asleep? I do still feel tired. My brother isn't home. The cops probably won't be back anytime soon. If no one's home. No one shook me awake. Why did I wake up at all? I check the time to reveal it's been about 2 hours.

Interesting.

I climb back into my bed and decided to go to sleep. To dream far away from here. Preferably a world with no problems. But a place like that doesn't exist. It never will. Someone please just make it end. Choose for me. Tell me that I don't have to worry or make a decision.

Chapter 19

I open my eyes to find myself on the table. This time with the elder physician. The other a man not quite as frail but rather muscular in build. There's no sight of anyone else.

"Well, hello there." he says.

I blink confused on how I ended back up here. I didn't do any painting, so I should've went into a normal sleep. I shouldn't be here in Asylo. What's happening.

"I-I-I don't know how I," I say babbling.

"Ended up here." he tells me "So soon. Well I do. Hmmm."

"Who are you?" I ask.

"Head Elder." he states.

"I'm Uvania." I say introducing myself.

"Nice to meet you. However, I must tell you some rather disturbing news. Your body won't be able to handle going back and forth much longer. You must choose between the two worlds. It's a hard decision to make. It's very hard indeed. But until you choose your spiritual body will continue to keep launching between here and the other side. When making the decision you will then go through the appropriate ritual. I hope you will make the right decision." He explains.

He doesn't tell me what the pros and cons are. He doesn't try to persuade me to stay or go. He doesn't tell me anything I didn't think of a moment ago. He only tells me that I am now being forced to make a decision. He's vague but in a polite way. I don't know why. But the two Elders are really sweet. They're starting to grow on me.

"I hope you will also make your decision before it's too late."

"Head Elder. We're ready." a boy says.

"Would you like to accompany us as we head out to find your friend?" The Head Elder invites me.

"Sure." I say.

Getting up from the table I notice my arm feels way better now. Definitely doesn't hurt like it did when I was home. The Head Elder guides me out of the physician's tent. I see the rest of the Peira all holding some type of weapon. Some none at all. But most of them yeah. Some hold cross bows or bows and arrows. Others carry bow staffs or spears. Some of them I don't even know what they are.

I look up at the Head Elder "I don't know why. But I was under the impression or I felt like the Peira were always pacifist."

"We are," he responds, "there is nothing wrong with intimidation though."

I don't know how much I believe that but I just nod.

"Alright people lets head out." The Elder announces.

The Peira begin to follow the boy I saw earlier. They all walk on command of the elder with no further instruction. I receive no further explanations. I don't ask either. I assume there's a reason for everything. If it's meant to be it will play out here. I realize I'm more calm and level headed to think this here in Athala. But this is how it is. I'm just along for the ride.

Around half an hour later of walking through snow the boy says Pippy is nearby. Keep an eye out. Whether it was intentional or not they all formed a very wide circle with their guard up. The Elder and I in the center. I'm having trouble distinguishing the Peira I had dreamed about and had all these ideals about them opposed to the hunters that stand before me.

"Halt!" the boy says bow and arrow ready to fire. The Elder and I walk over to see. Everyone coming in closer to see but remaining behind us. We stop 5 feet away from where the boy stands aimed ready to fire.

Pippy stands with his arms up beside his head. "I see you found me. Good job old man."

"We're not here to play games." the elder said. "Well you didn't come to kill me that's for certain. You believe in peace. Not violence." he says in somewhat of a mocking tone to the elder.

This is definitely not the side of Pippy that I know. Well maybe a bit on our last get together. But he seemed sweet at first. Then again, they always do don't they.

"Don't be so sure about that." Lilian walks up to him with her own bow and arrow pointed. Hers is made of metal and the arrow has a very fine sharpened point.

"Easy there Lilian," Pippy says as he gets down onto his knees in surrender "Let's not do anything we'll regret."

Lilian pulls her bow even further. You can see she's waiting so desperately yet patiently. Even with her bow drawn you can see a hint of her confliction on the situation.

"Plus, you wouldn't kill one of your own, would you?" Pippy says loud enough for everyone to hear.

"What is he talking about?" the Elder mumbles to himself.

"Watch. Everyone look at me. See for yourselves." Everyone stares at him. No one lets their guard down though. Pippy shuts his eyes. When they open he looks like one of us? Eyes pupil less clear as day. Not the slightest falter.

Everyone steps back in disbelief. Pippy begins to stand up.

"Don't get up," Lilian says not convinced "It's a trick I know it. You always did want to be one of us."

"I'm shocked Lilian. You don't trust me. After all we've been through."

"There is no we. Just you." she tells him.

"We're the same."

"You're not one of us." Lilian says through gritted teeth.

"Then how did he do it?" asks the Elder.

"I don't know."

"He had to have used magic. Something only the Peira could possibly do."

"If he could use magic like we could he would've escaped a long time ago. He wouldn't have needed the girl." she says angrily.

"There's only so much magic I can use" Pippy speaks up.

"We all used magic to trap him. It would be too dif-"

The Elder trails off his sentence and is interrupted by the sound of the metal arrow piercing straight through him. *It definitely hit the center of his rib cage and spinal cord in the process. Pippy's body is motionless at first. His body levitates from the ground blood dripping from his body. His body then trembles. Next thing I see is Lilian electrocuting Pippy continuously. Lightning spidering from her hands on to his weightless body. I focus on her. She seems so angry and upset.*

Her eyes aren't natural anymore. There is a lightning storm taking place. You can see the lightning strike. The dark gray clouds rolling. Everything else is just black. The lightning from her fingers starts to turn blue and purple, and every so often yellow.

"Why doesn't anyone stop her." I ask The Elder.

"She can't hear us. We can't stop her without suffering like he is right now. Advice. You never go to war with an angry person."

"I see."

Pippy's body disintegrates into black dust. Lilian comes out of her trance. No one says a word. Eventually when everything that has just taken place before my eyes is fully processed the elder gives the order to go back to the base. I notice that the members don't show any emotion about his death. Not happy to no longer have to worry about his death. Or sad about him dying like that. Or confused from his ways of using magic before their eyes. Simply just focusing on going back to base. Continuing on with their lives.

<u>Chapter 20</u>

We make it back to base and everyone let's their guard down completely throwing away their weapons into a cabinet I didn't quite notice earlier. When all the armory is in, its locked away with a key and padlock that only the Elders know.

Out of the corner of my eye I notice Lilian continues to walk. Where is she going? She seems sad and disappointed now. Not holding a front anymore, I see. Even a girl like her has capability of feeling something every now and again. What the elder told me seems to be true.

I decide to follow her. Running to catch up to her I stop by her side. She's dragging her feet through the snow. For someone who was so dead set on killing someone she surely seems upset and filled with regret over the situation. She was practically given an order to stand down. Which she herself, all on her own whim decided to defy. She chooses now to look and feel the consequences of her decision. "Where are you headed?" I ask lightly.

She responds with silence.

"If you don't tell me where we are headed I will just keep following you until we arrive." I say.

More silence.

She's really bummed out right now. I mean I get it. She totally has the blood on her hands for his death and no one is born a killer. But seriously her mood right now is highly contagious. I thought I was out of it earlier.

We continue walking for hours. The snow starts to peel away in this area and turns into trees instead of mountains. The air is less chilly than before. This part of the region is definitely more different. This part is more of a summer scene from a movie you would see on TV. Or at least something like it.

"Lilian, where are we?" I say a bit in wow.

Which I should be because I have a feeling that the others haven't been here before. If they had I'm sure they'd set up base here and not the freezing tundra there at now. It's strange. Why would she keep a place like this a secret?

"Your hiding something aren't you?" I say to her.

Her eyes remain fixated on the ground. Minutes later we approach a huge gathering of trees and bushes with flowers freshly bloomed and fruits that are ripe. She pushes them aside with them slightly resisting. I follow her through the small forest. I mean what could possibly be back here other than more trees, some bugs, and things that could possibly make me itchy. This better be worth it. I can't handle being itchy and given the cold

164

shoulder by someone I would deem as crazy and not to mention a bit rude as well as pushy.

She stops up ahead. I stand beside her for a better view. We are peering out over a very huge lake. Which is honestly a very strange color. I've never seen a pink lake before. Then again in the real world I haven't seen any. So maybe I should be saying I haven't heard of any pink lakes.

I look at Lilian and the lake. Is she going to explain any of this? Nothing is making sense. Which I see is going to be the story of my life. Me forever asking others to explain in great detail what is going on around me.

"It's my fault." She says.

"Okay." I say still confused.

"It's all my fault."

"Well yeah. You shot him with a metal arrow." I tell her.

"Not just that," she tells me "The whole thing. I was the reason he was banished. I shouldn't have gotten so close to him. I should've stopped while I was ahead. I knew he was becoming a bad apple and I did nothing to put an end to it."

"Lilian," I say in a serious tone "What did you do?"

"I taught him magic. I don't know how he discovered that he can actually do magic. I just know he was obsessed with it when he first was introduced to the clan and saw all of our abilities. When he showed me he had potential to do magic. I practically showed him everything he knows. I showed him how to turn magic into a deadly weapon." she looks at me.

She won't get an argument from me on that after the number she did on him. She literally fried him to bits and pieces.

"I didn't mean to really. The more I taught the more crazed he became with it," she continues "He was so happy. I loved seeing his smile. So, I didn't really notice at first." she trails off.

I wait for her to continue to the story as she just willingly tells me all this information. She still doesn't like me I'm sure. But she's made it quite obvious she can really use a friend. Or at least someone to talk to. Someone to, in a way, take Pippy's place.

"We came to the lake. We would hide here. One day we came here. We spent the entire day here. Told the others we were adventuring. We were young kids after all. It takes a lot of time to age in Athala. If you age at all. So, the others didn't mind. If we went on adventures, we would be out of their hair." she explains.

"I see."

"When we spent the entire day here we noticed the pink lake showed a reflection to the real world."

She points out to the lake as it starts to stir. At first slowly then gradually it begins to whirlpool. It starts to change colors. It even starts to bubble then settles. After a few minutes I see the reflection of the real world with my own eyes.

"We named the lake the looking glass," she begins "In the beginning that was all we used it for. Look at how the real world was changing. Watching people go about their day to day lives. It all started out so innocent."

"What happened," I say, "What changed?" "Over time we visited the lake more often. We wanted to learn all its mysteries. We learned we could interact with our magic on this side and control others on the other side," she begins "We use to do simple tricks. Making bunnies dance. Or just something funny. It was temporary. For fun and giggles. But then," she says changing to a more serious tone "Pippy. . .He wanted to do something more. Something bigger and less innocent than animals. Something that would-be life changing."

"Like what?" I say hoping she's not about to say what I'm already thinking.
"He wanted to create a perfect Utopia. I mean I knew he was adventurous but to me that was going too far. That's when he was crossing a very firm line. I finally saw how dangerous the lake could be. I saw how dangerous Pippy could be."

"So, you framed him." I say.

She nods giving me confirmation.

"If it's one thing we all wanted it was peace. Pippy and I never saw anyone actually interacting from the other end. But I figured it was only a matter of time before someone on the other side would find their own pink lake or looking glass. Things usually work both ways. So, I convinced the others that he was guilty of giving away our location. I didn't want anyone to believe Pippy. They wouldn't if he was deemed a traitor of the clan. Luckily the timing worked out. I never gave him a chance to tell anybody. I mean what if someone else came a long and wanted to create a Utopia. Athala is separated from the real world for the most part. I would assume with good reason."

"So, you wanted things to stay the same."

"Of course, I'm happy here. Everyone is happy here. Athala is a Utopia. So, when Pippy was banished to the hot wasteland I figured our problems where over. Until you came along. That's when I knew I had to kill him. Which I did. I killed him," she says nonchalant "For the greater good I suppose."

"I suppose so."

"With that being said." she says to me. Our eyes making direct eye contact. Firmly locked on each other.

"Will you keep my secret? Or do I have to kill you too."

About the Author

Oops! She accidentally became an author. Erin started off as a normal psychology major. Then one day she randomly decided to sit down and write her very first book. Between being in love with authors, wanting to be self-employed, discovering self-publishing, and wanting to share her creativity. She dived straight in.

To get started she took Neil Gaiman's quote to heart. "This is how you do it: you sit down at the keyboard and you put one word after another until its done. It's that easy, and that hard." So she did exactly that. Next thing she knew her very first book was born. Yes, this book your holding in your very own hands. Once she finished she decided to publish it for all the world to see.

After all, there was nothing stopping her.

Visit her at:
thewritersscene.com
facebook.com/ohsweetmomsen
twitter.com/ohsweetmomsen
Instagram: @OhSweetMomsenAuthor
@TheWritersScene